THE MAN

VALERIE

To all who love reading

Thanks to Mark for editing

CONTENTS

Chapter 1: 'What is thy sentence then but speechless death?'

Chapter 2: 'Nor shall death brag thou wander'st in his shade'

Chapter 3: 'A man can die but once'

Chapter 4: 'The miserable have no other medicine, only hope'

Chapter 5: 'The robb'd that smiles, steals something from the thief'

Chapter 6: 'Speak less than thou knowest'

Chapter 7: 'Time shall unfold what plighted cunning hides'

Chapter 8: ' 'Tis best to weigh the enemy more mighty than he seems'

Chapter 9: 'I say there is no darkness but ignorance'

Chapter 10: 'Come not between the dragon and his wrath'

Chapter 11: 'Why then tonight let us assay our plot'

Chapter 12: 'It's not enough to speak, but to speak true'

Chapter 13: 'Some rise by sin, and some by virtue fall'

Chapter 14: 'The fault, dear Brutus, is not in our stars but in ourselves'

NAMED PLAYERS

MYRES ISLAND

Judith Pendleton	*Island resident*
Gail Hanworth	*Friend of Judith*
Jack	*Island resident*
Geoff Hardwicke	*Landlord of 'The Ship Inn'*

BRITISH POLICE

Superintendent Andrew Foale

CID:

Detective Chief Inspector Brian Hammond
Detective Inspector John Bridgeworth
Detective Sergeant Alan Woodley
Detective Constable Harry Brier
Detective Constable Sian Ross

OCU:

Detective Inspector Robert Matthews
Detective Sergeant Chris Harris
Detective Sergeant Caroline Kemble

LONDON

Graham Birch

Jake Harrison	*Colleague of Graham*
Margaret Birch	*Mother of Graham*
Josie Gillespie	*Sister of Graham*
Mrs Godwin	*Landlady of guest house*
Alice	*Joint manager of Mary House*
Grace	*Joint manager of Mary House*
Thomas Uckley	*Legal counsel*

OCG

Jakub Rusu
Gregor Rusu
Andrei Vulpe
Radek Janota
Anton Masin
Josef

'Hana'
Frank Beckswith
PRAGUE
Captain Bucek   *Chief of Police*
Officer Kostelcky
Johanna de Hoek
Jan de Hoek   *Brother of Johanna*
Matyas   *Support worker*
Simecek   *Contact*
AMSTERDAM
Chief Constable Visser   *Chief of Police*

CHAPTER ONE   *'What is thy sentence then but*
speechless death?'   (Thomas Mowbray, *Richard II*)
He should have known.

The man trembled, as he grasped the iron bar.
He should have known, he shouldn't have been stupid …

He walked forward, away from the men waiting at the truck. Dusk was bringing a heavy odorous mist, and the evening traffic was building on the motorway. Lookouts at the entrance to the lockup space hunched against the damp. City detritus was scattered around, wet and stagnant.

The man drew a key from his jacket, clenched it in his free fist and approached the garage door.

He turned to the men. 'Stay back, keep a look out.'

He approached the door, and raised the bar in his right hand slowly.

He should have known … so he should be dead … he deserved to die …

He unlocked the padlock and moved swiftly to the side. There was no sound.

He waited.

He should be dead … he deserved to die …

As the door rolled up, the man's eyes took moments to adapt to the darkness. Closest to the door were heaps of indeterminate metal, plastic bowls, empty paint tins. As his eyes adjusted, he saw piles of rags which had migrated to the far corners of the garage.

One pile, on the left hand side at the back, was rounder, more solid than the rest. He knew. He breathed deeply, and felt relieved and shamed, in that one breath.

He called to the men.

'He's here. Get the doors open.'

They dragged out the body, of what would have been a youngish man, now with skin tinged pale blue-green, eyes beneath closed lids sunken inwards, jaw loose and fixed, like a skull. It looked as if he had slipped awkwardly to one side, as if he had fallen asleep – but then had died instead. They ripped out the contents of his belt pouch. The men cleared up the paraphernalia they had left with the man. Syringes, but no water or food, for seven days.

The ancient island was always beautiful. It may not have the romance of the south west coast, or the bracing adventure of the north western isles, and was certainly not known for its entertainments, but its beauty survived, through all seasons, with the right eye – and clothes – and with the patience to quietly wait and watch for the sand martins in the coves, or a barn owl soaring over the saltmarshes. Turnstones foraged along the sea edge and occasionally families of grey and common seal appeared along the coastline. It was both a quietly dignified and cheerfully unpretentious place. Its location on the border of the North Sea with the English Channel and the Thames Estuary further south gave it a bleakness, chill, drama and unpredictability that made it hypnotic. It lived in anticipation of the encroaching sea finally swallowing the edge of the land, but meanwhile human life could be found in the seafarers' pubs and the ramshackle huts selling beach toys and fresh seafood. The peace came from the long, solitary excursions to be taken on foot around the island, breathing in the isolation, the dominance of nature and the sense of constant change, as the sea relentlessly challenged the fragile coastline. Heading out for a walk, even initially for a stroll, took the walker not only further down unexpected paths and through changing habitats, but to horizons which made distant shorelines further south seem close but remote, as the perspective of the sea shifted, like a mirage.

Access was along a causeway, which at new and full moon in the colder months was covered with the sea, separating the island from the mainland. In winter, islanders were used to building on their resilience and self-sufficiency to keep their lifestyles comfortable.

There wasn't really a trend for crime on the island, even though police services were based some miles away on the mainland. Most of the residential areas, in the west of the island, were modest, while those premises that were high end were well protected – and the risk of being cut off by the tide made most crime a fairly risky business, with no guarantee of the outcome being worth the challenge. Serious crime was rare, and mostly the island thrived on income from both its summer business, and fairly easy commuting routes to mainland towns. The sea, however, presented in contrast an opportunity for a different type of crime, with access by seacraft a possibility that some were prepared to undertake, and while it had been a prominent route of illicit access from the times of the Saxons and Romans, and through the peak of the smuggling industry, still it presented an opportunity which was open to the skilled sailor, who knew how to subvert the powers of the Channel authorities.

No-one on the island really started the average day worrying about crime. No-one expected the island to become embroiled in weeks of mystery, upheaval and fear following the events of the late summer.

....

Gail loved this journey. Although she could have driven, she felt it was more of an adventure to take the train from London to the nearest town to the island, just eight miles away, then take a taxi to the mainland end of the causeway and walk across to the island. It felt as if she was walking into the past, becoming part of the environment, breathing in the marshy air, the mix of mud and salt, listening to the unique sound of the distant sea and sensing the illusion of being far away from the cities, in place and time. She had come to visit her old friend, Judith, who now lived on the island, in comfortable early retirement, and a fellow walker of long shared history. Every time she visited, Gail felt firstly a burst of positivity, that it seemed she could live just as happily on the island forever, followed by the sense of reality which reminded her that she had a life in the city, which was ever changing and new, and full of possibilities. The island was great, she felt, for a little self-delusion, but just for a while.

Judith was busy whitewashing her scullery. Born in the 1950s, her nostalgia for adapted period décor had become a passion. There was, though, no freezing outside lavatory, or a big boiler used to wash bedsheets with the help of starch, a dolly blue bag, wooden tongs and a lethal mangle, all memories from her post-war childhood. In those days, the chickens and rabbits were kept for food, not companionship. She remembered the sound of the coalman filling the coal shed next to the outhouse, scary and big with his leather hood and shoulder cowl; the beautiful, gentle, huge, piebald horse pulling the greengrocer's cart, having a munch from her nosebag and tolerating cautious face scratches from toddlers held up in their mother's arms, while the greengrocer stopped for a chat and a sale. The rag and bone man rattled down the street with his noisy cartload of scrap, and bath time after school was in a zinc tub in front of a smoky, sparking fire. And, of course, there was discrimination, social exclusion, casual abuse and the post-war breakdown of infrastructure. These days, modern life was maybe not as slow and communal, but was clean, functional and exotic. Mass produced décor may be cheap and short-lived, but no longer did the deal dining table sport lace placemats and plastic daffodils which had been given free with boxes of soap powder.

Judith put down the ancient brush and greeted her old friend. They had begun school together, in the days when children didn't properly start school until they were five, had continued into their grammar school days, had a few teenage breakups and eventually went separate ways, Judith to train as a teacher and Gail to go to university and study pharmacy. Both had married, and both had been divorced. Judith had two children, Gail had none – which may have meant she was freer to expand in her career and geographically, while Judith stayed on the path expected of married women in the sixties and seventies. The differences led to longer separation, but intermittent contact, an almost lifelong friendship that survived the immediacy and fragility of modern relationships.

And now they met up often, usually on the island, but occasionally in Birmingham, where Gail now taught. It was the time on the island, however, that was companionable, predictable.

Usually there would be a walk planned. This time, they had decided to take on the long walk around the island, which usually took up most of the day, allowing for a late start, a relaxed pace, fairly frequent refreshment breaks and visits to the more remote parts of the island, not usually frequented by visitors. The weather outlook was reasonable, with cloud and an easterly breeze, but dry. The ground had warmed through the summer and now the worst of the mud had settled into hard ridges.

They took the coast road, and soon found themselves on the sea wall, passing the drainage polders, with the salt marsh to the left, increasing in visual depth to the sea line. A scattering of dykes and mud pools dotted the marshes, creating a pattern of shifting ecosystems, as hidden creatures created tiny eddies and quiet splashes in the shallow waters, the only interruption to the stillness. They paused to gaze across to the sea, allowing their senses to adjust to the sounds and smells of the marsh; herring gulls calling like sirens overhead and the tackle on the masts of distant moorings clinking like nautical wind chimes.

'Is that a seal over there?' Gail peered across the marsh.

'I wouldn't have thought so – it wouldn't be that far away from the water's edge. And it looks bigger than a seal … maybe old tarp, or sailcloth? You'd be amazed what washes up.'

'Maybe … It looks odd … perhaps we'll see it better if we walk up a bit …'

They moved on further, and the shape became clearer, elongated.

'Judith, I think it's a person …'

'What? I think you may be right – can you call emergency services? If it's a person, they're in trouble. Stay here, I'll go down and have a look.'

Judith returned, splashed with mud to the knees of her jeans, her face pale.

'He's dead, Gail. I think he's been there a while. What did you say on the phone?'

'I said we could see someone lying on the marshes, they said they're on their way, to ring back if we have any more information.'

'Can you ring them again? Can you tell them it's a man, he's dead, looks like for some time. Make sure police are on their way as well as an ambulance. We'd better wait here till they get here.'

…….

Judith and Gail were back at the cottage, Judith pouring out two glasses of whisky.

'I don't …' began Gail.

'You do now.' Judith placed a glass in her hand. 'Just take a sip. It'll lift you up a bit.'

'What did the police say?'

'They've cordoned off the beach, and they're going to come and see us shortly – I think they just want to check our details, that sort of thing. Meanwhile, take a break, I think some food would be a good idea. I'll sort something.'

…….

DI Bridgeworth's team were convened in the investigation room.

'Update please, DS Woodley.'

'White male, approximately 30-40 years of age, initial account from police surgeon is possibly death by drowning, probably more than a few days ago. To be confirmed or further clarified by PM. Found at approximately 11.00 a.m. on 2nd September by two females walking along the sea wall. They noticed what looked like a person lying on the beach and Mrs Hanworth called the emergency services. Mrs Pendleton was the only one of the two to approach the body and she confirmed she did not move or touch the body in any way. She informed her companion who relayed a second call to emergency services. Neither was able to identify the individual. Currently no initial information regarding fingerprint, DNA or dental identification yet, sir.'

'Nothing on the body?'

'No passport or other ID. Badly damaged belt pouch, contents must have been lost in the tides; it was open, nothing inside. Some old injuries to the face, according to CS.'

'Get the pouch to forensics, just in case there's anything worth knowing from it. Anything further from the two witnesses?'

'They were interviewed at Mrs Pendleton's home and confirmed that they had not seen anything further of interest, no other persons in the vicinity, no other unusual behaviour, sir. Mrs Pendleton is an island resident and is very familiar with the daily routine of the island. She said she hasn't heard of any attempts to land at that site.'

'Have we got any evidence of recent criminal activity relating to illegal landings in the area?'

'Not in the last year, sir.'

'Missper?'

'Working on that at the moment, sir.'

'What's known about drugs activity in the area?'

'Nothing directly related to individuals who have dealings on the island, sir. Most of that is a bit further south, the resorts on the mainland.'

'Right, in the absence of any new evidence, we want to focus on getting an identity. I want the PM report as soon as possible. Once we've got that, it's the usual search; forensics, fingerprints, DNA, dental, missing persons. Might have to think about overseas connections. Let's keep an eye on the area for anything else. Find out about any craft washed up, anything that might have come from a boat, anything unusual. In that sort of place, the locals usually have a weather eye on anything out of the ordinary. Oh, speak to the coastguards. Any door to door?'

'On that now, sir.'

'Good, but keep it low key. Just any unusual activity, anything out of the ordinary. Don't mention a body, or if *they* do, say the usual. Ongoing investigation, looking into it, so on. We can't get an e-FIT yet. The odds are this is either a dealer who's been on the wrong side of a rival, or an immigration attempt. But first we need to know if anyone is missing, if there's any possible ID that way.'

....

'It's them illegal immigrants, isn't it? One of those boat people, or something?'

'We don't have any information as to the identity of the person yet, sir. We're just seeing if anyone on the island might know if anyone has gone missing, or has seen anything unusual in the last few days?'

'I ain't seen nothin'. I go down to The Ship of a Friday night, keep to meself other'ns. If anyone would know, it would be Geoff at The Ship. He sees who comes and goes.'

'And you're not aware of anyone you maybe haven't seen for a while, a tradesman, neighbours, something like that?'

'As I said, nobody. I'm keepin' away from the shore at night though, you don't know what's goin' on down there.'

'Thank you for your time, sir. If you do see or hear of anything …'

'I'll let you'ns know.'

…….

'So what do you think it's about then, Jack?'

The Ship was as lively as it was normally of a Friday evening.

'It's one of them immigrants, in't it? Have you had the police round yet? I had one round yesterday, right up 'imself he was, but they don't know anythin' a'course. I bet you anythin' it's an illegal.'

'Someone's son, as they say. Feel sorry for the fella. What a way to go. Another one?'

'No, I'm headin' home. I don't like bein' out this time of the night. You can't trust them illegals, bound to be more …'

…….

'PM's in, sir.'

''What's the SP?'

'Male, probably European, age between around 35 to 40. Cause of death could not be determined conclusively as the male was already dead before he entered the water. Confirmed that cause was not drowning. Injuries to face pre-dated death, were maybe a couple of weeks old and wouldn't have been expected to be fatal. No signs of associated facial bone injuries, no skull fractures, no evidence of significant brain injury. No signs of significant haemorrhage before death, no wounds to the rest of the body. Owing to the condition, evidence from any defence injuries, stomach contents, bloods is inconclusive. No gross disease in any organs. Pathologist is going to get some further work done on the tissues. But medically, not clear, as it stands. No jewellery, watch, any other possessions on the body, clothes were largely damaged, but he appeared to have been dressed in outdoor clothing, several layers. No shoes or boots, as usual under the circumstances. But there were some possible identifying signs on the body. He was missing two incisors, but the rest of the dentition was healthy, well cared for, not so common with spontaneous loss of teeth apparently. He was missing the third and fourth fingers of his right hand – again, may have been the result of an accident. Pathologist said these were fairly recent and showed signs they had been crudely treated, maybe wrapped up, so not congenital. No signs of clinical repair to the hand, no sutures. Some possible puncture marks, but difficult to distinguish, as there was the usual blood pooling, difficult to separate from bruising. He had tattoos – a wolf's head behind his right shoulder, and – here's the icing on the cake – on his left arm, the word *svoboda*.'

'OK, go for it, I know you want to.'

'Czech for freedom.'

'Czech? That's not the usual – Serbian, Albanian maybe – but Czech? But you're right, that's a bit of a bonus. Maybe. Looks like we're in it for the long haul. Fingerprints?'

'Nothing on our database, sir, but we haven't yet used CPNI.'

'While we're waiting for forensics then, we'd better start with looking at any contacts we're currently aware of. We need to look at everything we know about organisation of forced labour, trafficking, slavery, known felons associated with cartels, anything that might suggest reasons for someone trying to get into the country illegally, or being forced to. Was he a mule? Was that pouch connected with that? Bit small for anything significant. It looks as if we might be going that way. But we need much more – chase up the full forensics.'

…….

DI Bridgeworth looked at the scene. It wasn't always particularly useful to go to the scene of the crime, but in this case he wanted to see if anything stood out to him, just from a visual. To his slight disappointment, there was no sign indicating what had happened, or why. It was cold, grey, drizzly and muddy. This was a bit of a depressing place. He found the location of the discovery of the body and looked out to sea. So where did the body come from? They would usually wash up in Kent, the closest point to the continent. Not damaged enough to have just drifted this far up from the Channel - it would have taken days, surely. So where from? What ships or boats came this way? Was it dumped off a craft? Was it coming from further north, Belgium, Netherlands, even Denmark? If from further north up the English coast itself, surely it would have washed up before now? How far was the Czech Republic from the coast? He searched on his phone, peered at a blurred map and calculated roughly that the direct route from there to Britain was through to the north of France via Germany and Belgium, but that the Netherlands were technically opposite the east coast of Britain. He felt the old, familiar, obsessive itch which wouldn't let him shift from maybe the Netherlands, and possibly specifically Amsterdam. That would surely be a key location. He couldn't get rid of it until he'd got back to the office and booked the tickets.

…….

'We haven't really got a clear link yet, sir.'

'I know. We're opening it up to Interpol. I just want to get the feel. I've okayed it, we need to follow up the possibility that the individual is from the Czech Republic, came across Europe to the Netherlands, and if he's not, well, then we might be able to eliminate that route. Let's face it, we haven't actually got anything yet. There may be information we can get through other channels. We can access the forensic report on our way.'

'Sorry, sir, but I just wonder if we ought to tie up …'

'As I said, DS Woodley, we can catch up with anything on the way. You can use WiFi on planes now, you know. We will have the information we need and can move on from there.'

'Right, sir. I'll get ops to sort it out, sir.'

'Prague, then Amsterdam. I've contacted their police departments; we just need to book in the times.'

'On it, sir.'

CHAPTER TWO   *'Nor shall death brag thou wander'st in his shade.'*   (*Sonnet 8*)

They were approaching the runway for Vaclar Havel airport. DI Bridgeworth was checking through paperwork and preparing documentation for the police.

'We're seeing Captain Bucek, at the Department of Foreign Police – they have provided a car, driven by an Officer … er, Kostelcky, I think. I've sent the dental and DNA results through. I've spoken to the Captain – he said that he has information he wants to talk about in more depth. Let's see what Prague has to offer us.'

In less than half an hour they had arrived at the offices of the Department of Foreign Police. The streets of Prague were decorated with unrestrained - and apparently unmanaged - graffiti, mostly in Czech but sometimes in English, proclaiming freedom. There was a restless air of social pride combined with evidence of harder, brutal times. Pockets of the past were seen in the presence of the older residents: the women in cotton headscarves, traditionally dressed in black, sometimes with brown linen aprons; the men fiercely staking their ground outside roadside bars, pipe-smoking, sitting in companionable silence, and making their Pravha beer last the afternoon. Charles Bridge, surging with tourists, was colourful, haphazard and discordant.

The police building, in contrast, was square and featureless, more like a block of flats or a budget hotel than a police department, but inside was modern and cool. They waited at the entrance while a polite and deferential young officer checked their identification and called his superior to confirm their appointment.

Captain Bucek welcomed them courteously.

'Thank you for making the journey, Detective Inspector. I hope you will find the visit of some value, although we would have been happy to share what we can in the normal way.'

'I thought it would be useful to get a feel for the environment we're considering in this case, sir. As you have seen from the evidence we have been able to examine in the UK, our forensic team has not been able to establish the identity of the victim. We have reason to believe the individual had some connection with Eastern European locations. We want to do all we can to clarify whether we are dealing with a crime, whether it is domestic or international. If we get to a point where we can go no further, then it will have to be a case of person unknown. We get enough of those. But as I explained to you over the phone, he does not appear on any database we are able to access in Britain, and if we are able to get closer to identifying his background, then we might be able to at least inform the relevant organisations.'

'We have, as you say, the good news, and the bad news. Or maybe it's all bad news, I'm afraid. The DNA records do not come up on our database, nor the fingerprints, or the e-FIT. But that would only suggest that this individual is not known to our police. If there is any good news, we have what might be, I suppose, incidental information. The tattoos are interesting, if not conclusive – the word '*svoboda*' does not only mean freedom – it is quite a common surname in Czechia, I suppose equivalent to your Freeman. So you might be looking at a man with the surname Svoboda, or someone who supports freedom, or someone who has had the name tattooed on as a kind of sign of ownership by another – and in conjunction with the other information – the wolf's head tattoo, and the absence of two fingers on the right hand, we may be then looking down a more sinister route.

'Prague is a known transit point for criminal activities such as human trafficking, and forced labour, particularly amongst the Roma community, who spread freely across the Eastern European countries, often difficult to track or identify. After political corruption, and bribery, it is probably our biggest challenge, bearing in mind that the illegal drugs trade is tied up with all of these problems. *Podzim* – it means autumn – presumably an ironic counter to the Prague Spring – is a group which controls much of this activity through infiltration at the highest – and lowest – levels. There is still resistance to many of the changes that have taken place in Eastern Europe since the end of the second World War. They appear to be concerned to reassert the power of the autocracy and restore control over freedoms and identity. They fund themselves very substantially by involvement in the transit activities. Disclosure of any of their activities results in immediate and brutal retaliation, usually in the form of murder, preceded by torture. The first act is to remove the third and fourth fingers of the right hand - as a kind of warning, or guarantee against further indiscretions.'

'So you think there is a possibility that this individual was a member of this group?'

'That would be very hard to say on the basis of such superficial evidence. But the word *svoboda* is more likely to mean freedom than someone's surname, if it was a voluntary tattoo, and the wolf's head is a common symbol of reactionary groups, who form resistance bodies against the organisation.'

'So he could have been fighting against *Podzim*?'

'Or an infiltrator, or indeed a perpetrator, or a collaborator. It is not uncommon for individuals to use a cover to enable them to inveigle themselves into the resistance groups. And the other way round. Information is powerful and useful to both sides. It is sometimes impossible to identify the role of any given individual on the database of individuals known to be involved in the activity.'

'Does that take us any further?'

'I'm afraid I'm guessing that it doesn't. The best it can suggest is that he may speak Czechian. Everything else is circumstantial.'

'When you say that Prague is a transit point – where do the goods – or people – get moved to?'

'It can be further east, to Russia, Romania and Serbia particularly – but more usually it is west, towards Germany, the Netherlands, Britain – it is easier to control that way than risk engagement with the many subversive cells in the other direction. And in any case, the - shall we say - richest source of supply comes from those more turbulent areas to the east, where security and controls are much looser.'

'What about missing persons?'

Captain Bucek glanced out of the window and paused.

'I am very sorry, Detective Inspector. Without something concrete - the possibility of cross-checking some identification - it would be completely impossible. We have many, many individuals who never appear on any government system. They stay in the hinterland of society. I assure you it is very unlikely that the individual you have discovered would have been traceable through any normal circumstances.'

'The body was found off the east coast of Britain and hadn't been in the sea for more than a few days at most. The Dutch coast would be much closer than the French. Will it be worth our while to travel to Amsterdam, would we gain anything by that?'

'Chief Constable Visser is the Head of Police there, and is very involved in gathering information which might help to address the trafficking issue in the country, particularly in Amsterdam and the ports. He may actually have something more direct for you, as his city is so close to key physical transit locations. But I'm afraid he is quite difficult to access. I can call him, to see if her would give you some time. It really depends whether he knows anything more about the potential identity or role of your victim. I'm afraid I suspect he may not. If he was in a position to do so, he may be prepared to see you, but this is one of many cases that are likely not to be solved. There should be an international drive to track down and contain these dreadful activities, but sadly resources are not always readily available. I am so sorry we cannot help you any further.'

'I appreciate your time, Captain Bucek. I won't take up more. We need to find an overnight stop here to pull everything together, and get a flight in the morning.'

'Please, our department is happy to provide accommodation, and has booked you two rooms at one of our finest hotels, at our expense. It's a beautiful Art Deco building directly opposite our famous Astronomical Clock. You will be very comfortable there, and fortunately as it is now midweek you won't have too much disturbance from our many celebrating visitors. You can work quietly there and prepare for your trip to Amsterdam. I would be ashamed not to give you the opportunity to enjoy a little of our Prague hospitality.'

'That's extremely generous, Captain. Thank you. I will let you know if we find anything that may be of value to you.'

The *Vevoda* was impressive, and based in the centre of the Old Town, just off the historic Square, in a narrow street busy with tourist shops and entrancing Romanesque buildings. Each evening the street would be littered with the detritus of visitor activity, which was cleared smartly away by the early morning street cleaning trucks. The quietly grand street entrance to the *Vevoda* led to a cool, silent and elegant foyer. Bridgeworth noted that the corners of the walls were carefully encased in ornate bronze guards to protect them from the hustle and bustle of suitcases and revellers, in the guise of presenting an impression of opulence. The period lift was heavy and elaborate but fitted with up-to-date electronic controls. Original paintings on the wall struck the right tone between classical and contemporary. Everything was exotic but tasteful.

The heated rooftop restaurant gave a view over autumnal Prague which blended history and fantasy. It oversaw red roofed buildings and fairy tale towers, and countless lights produced sparkling, dancing images over the water of the romantic Vltava, reinforcing the sense of timelessness. Smart, young Czechians in their white shirts and black waistcoats moved with skill and quiet efficiency around the restaurant, balancing courtesy with intimacy as they served the meals graciously. The food was astonishing and the wine sublime. It would form a dramatic contrast to the kind of hospitality that the British police would, in anyway rare circumstances, offer to visiting colleagues, it occurred to DI Bridgeworth. A Premier Inn would be excessive. He made a mental note to remember to send an appropriate acknowledgement when they returned – nothing to be lost by keeping up good international relations.

…….

The exposure of Prague as a covert transit point for the worst of crimes seemed not to provide any way forward. Amsterdam may be different.

'I'm afraid Chief Constable Visser is unable to see you.'
The officer at the entrance desk of the Police Headquarters in Amsterdam spoke perfect English, was polite and official, but carefully showed no sign of interest.
'I had hoped that Captain Bucek of Prague would have spoken to him.'
The woman breathed a quiet and measured sigh. Still the eyes looked but didn't see.
'I can't speak for Chief Constable Visser's decisions, sir. I suggest you request a meeting formally by letter.'
'I see. Is there anyone I could speak to here?'
The woman suppressed a proprietorial smile.
'If you need to speak to a police officer regarding a criminal matter, you are welcome to wait until one is available.'
The impasse was clear, and the two men left to find somewhere quiet, to plan their next steps.
They headed out on their return to the airport and stopped in the café culture area near the De Wallen region. Away from the lively, fragrant riverside life of hipster cafes they found a small restaurant down a narrow street, populated with cyclists and overshadowed by tall, narrow Dutch Colonial buildings housing a mix of homes and shops, which was suddenly and surprisingly still and quiet.
There was an air of steamy coolness, as the bustling restaurants stepped up their business in the rather chill, weak midday sunlight. The nearest seemed to be staffed by a solitary woman, relaxed and familiar, who came over to their table. Like many, she spoke excellent English, and was happy to regale them with not only what she had to offer, but also what they should and shouldn't do in Amsterdam.
'Always go to a restaurant – a café means something a little different here. We don't have that kind of service. I like to see English people, they always want tea and pastries, not what you get in the cafés.'

She clearly felt she had a duty to distance herself from the relaxed drug culture and was possibly trying to protect these respectable gentlemen from the wickedness of the city – innocently unaware that probably they saw more cannabis in their average working week than she did.

'As long as you two gentlemen avoid the more … obvious … areas, keep your possessions close, you will be fine. This is a beautiful city, you know. We have maps at the counter if you would like one.'

'Thank you, we're fine. Do you have much trouble here, then?'

'Not in this part of the city, sir, although of course if you're not into the café activities you would do well to avoid a lot of the places where there might be more risk, pickpocketing, mugging, that sort of thing. I recommend the nice places – we have some wonderful museums, Van Gogh, Anne Frank …'

'Unfortunately, we are on a flying visit, but thank you. Maybe there'll be a chance to do that another time. We'll just have a couple of coffees for now, if you would.'

The woman, disappointed but politely accepting, quickly served their coffees and took their payment, before spotting another respectable, possibly English, couple, who must surely appreciate advice for their visit to Amsterdam.

'I think we can't really do very much here, Woodley. Without access to the police, and without the jurisdiction to investigate the criminal population, I can't see how we can move things forward. We'll get back to the office and decide where we go from here. I don't think we can justify spending much more time on this, unless something comes up that changes what we've got, which is not a great deal at the moment. We have a picture of widespread criminal activity across Europe which seems difficult to pin down, as if we didn't know that already, which this individual may or may not be a part of. We've got nothing either way. We need to get back and see if we can find anything which links with this *Podzim* group – I'm not inclined to think that the wolf's head tattoo and the missing fingers are completely coincidental. Make a note that I want to speak to the pathologist again when we get back. Can anything of the injury to the hand indicate how the fingers were lost? I don't know if that will make any difference. I want to check missing persons again, especially as now we may potentially have a surname. Can we check with forensics again as well – is there anything with facial recognition tech that can take us any further? Long shots, but you never know.'

Losing interest in trying to find accommodation – after the *Vevoda*, anything else that was in the budget would be a depressing disappointment – they managed to get tickets for a late flight to London and booked a taxi.

CHAPTER THREE   *'A man can die but once.'*   (Feeble, *Henry IV Part 2*)

'We might have to park this for a bit, Woodley.'

The two officers were reviewing the previous few days, and the updated reports.

'So, we've got more from forensics – the fingers were removed by a clean cut, as if by a hatchet, but also could be caused by machinery of some kind. Facial recognition has not produced any relevant information. Teeth loss was not caused by disease, but injury as from a blow can't be ruled out. The pouch was about 20 cm square in size, leather, attached by a strap of similar material, difficult to identify any contents owing to water submersion over several days. It had a catch which had been ripped off, which could have been caused by anything. We know the facial injuries were at least a week or so old, were broadly contusions and abrasions, difficult to discriminate from the effects of water submersion, again could have been caused by accident or by assault.

'From comms, coastguards confirmed they had not had reports of any damage to or loss of craft, or of any risk to life incidents, in the couple of weeks before the discovery of the body. NCA had given us some intel on *Podzim*. They have cells throughout Europe and probably here in the UK, but are a relatively small organisation, presumably because they prefer to work on the premise that there is danger in numbers, rather than the opposite. They rely heavily on the use of small-time negotiators and facilitators, who arrange for the physical transport of people and goods on the basis of silence and payment – they don't get involved in direct contact. Apparently a lot of these are treated as expendable, you might say. The next level up are the carriers. Most of these live in the narrow belt of unofficial anonymity that enables them to keep moving. Simply, it's difficult to pin down any one specific person, unlike with the big cartels, which makes the whole business surprisingly successful.

'At the top are those who create the opportunities – the fake passports, the fake jobs and accommodation – in return for the substantial proceeds of slavery, of some kind or another. In order to keep the system stable, they deal with risky individuals extremely quickly. Speculation can take us down the path of thinking that this man was a victim of this process, but on the other hand the evidence is very circumstantial. He may still have also been at the sharp end of proceedings. Or he may be completely unconnected.

'And nothing from missing persons if the surname is correct.

'I think an inquest will definitely put it down as an unexplained death, and it will be dealt with in the normal way. We'll hold it for the moment. We've had something come in, closer to home, which we need to work on. I wouldn't spend too much time looking any more into our man for now but keep it near the top of the pile. Keep alert to anything similar, especially if it's associated with the location of the discovery of the body. Check in with NCA to confirm it's still technically an open case. Meanwhile, we have to look at something that has come up – definitely a murder this time. Body of a man has been found at the side of the A120, just south of the airport. Straightforward stabbing, it looks like. SOC have cleared the site, there isn't much we can do by going down there, so we'll get the SP from uniform and start a file. Could you go over to ops and get the investigation going?'

....

DS Woodley put his coffee down and leaned forward over the desk.

'What have we got then, Harry?'

DC Brier opened a document and shared the contents, photographs of the victim and the crime scene.

'Chap identified as Graham Birch from his driving licence, found in his jacket pocket. 32 year old male, UK resident, white British, born in Swindon. Was resident in South London. Wallet contained credit and debit cards, around £40 in cash, sports club membership card. Had a vehicle registered in his name but this was not present at the scene. Vehicle was later found burned out in a field near Hanningfield. Car contained a carrier bag with bottled water, some snacks, a supermarket receipt, matched with the debit card. There was a sports bag in the boot, containing trainers, a towel, shower gel, some gym kit. Cause of death was exsanguination due to injury from four stab wounds to the upper chest and neck, with a weapon thought to be a knife, forensics are clarifying that. There was no weapon present at the scene. Forensics are doing fingerprints, DNA. He was wearing jeans, trainers, a green and red rugby shirt and a grey lightweight jacket. Family have been informed and are being interviewed. He was single, lived alone, worked as a systems analyst.'
'So we need to start getting information about his lifestyle, work colleagues, any friends, any contacts. Speak to the gym. Catch up with forensics. Look for any financial concerns, debts, loans. Check with pathology, any health issues, any other injuries. Check with the family interviews – do we need to follow up anything there? Has he got a partner, girlfriend, boyfriend? Any rivals? As his cards and cash weren't taken, I don't think this was a straightforward robbery, at the moment, unless the perpetrator was looking for something specific. See if you can find out if there was any evidence that anyone was in the car with him. We need to get this done as soon as possible and get a CPS case put together. I'm interested in the family, first of all.'
…….
'We realise this is a very difficult conversation for you both. I understand you, Mrs Birch, are Graham's mother, and you are his sister, Josie … Gillespie?'

'That's correct.'

'You understand that Graham's body was found at the roadside, and that his car had been found burnt out at some distance away. He also had injuries which were consistent with a violent attack, and not as the result of a collision or by his own hand. I'm sorry this information is distressing, but we must make it clear that we are treating this as a murder enquiry, and not an accident.'

Josie Gillespie sat perched on the edge of the armchair in the smart but slightly dated suburban bungalow, arms and legs crossed. She occasionally glanced down at her clenched hands, or out of the window, making little eye contact with her mother, but fixing her gaze defiantly on the officers. She appeared somewhat out of place in the neat and ordered environment – casually dressed in rather grubby jeans and a white crop top, long, jet black hair in a tangled bun. Her mother sat apart from her, in a green chintz armchair by the net curtains of the window, her gaze fixed on the police officers.

'We get it, inspector. I would prefer to answer any questions if I can, to spare my mother the stress.'

'Of course. But it may be necessary to hear any information from your mother that may be of importance. When was the last time either of you saw Graham?'

'We were both present at the time. It was Thursday evening. He came over to drop off some decorating materials - I'm doing up the back bedroom. He was in a hurry, didn't stay to eat. He said he was going to drive up to Cambridge the next day, to see a colleague. The next we heard was on Saturday morning, after he had been found.'

'Was he in contact at all on Friday?'

'Not with either of us. He might have been in touch with work at some point, though. The company is Ledger Bankside Holdings.'

'What do you know of Graham's work associates, friends, anyone else who might have been in touch with him? Any partner?'

'Not with work colleagues – oh, apart from Jake – Harrison. They worked a lot together on projects, I think. He mentioned a woman a while ago, I don't know if she was a work colleague. Jane, I think he said. He led a very separate life from ours, though, on the whole. He seemed to be very involved with his work.'

'Hobbies?'

'He was a bit of a fitness freak, liked working out. Otherwise, I don't know.'

'Would you happen to have any contact details, phone numbers, of anyone connected with him?'

'No – as I said, Graham kept himself to himself. Not deliberately, I imagine – he was just a bit of a workaholic.'

'Mrs Birch, would you like to add anything?'

'No – what Josephine says sums it up really. We didn't see much of him.'

'Did you have any concerns about his lifestyle, any work pressures, that sort of thing?'

'As Josephine said, he lived a very separate life. He didn't confide in us.'

'Is there anything either of you would like to ask us at the moment?'

Josie looked up.

'What will happen to his body?'

'It won't be long before we have finished any investigations we need to make regarding Graham's body. But I'm afraid it can't be released until we have completed our enquiries and the case can be closed, pending the results of an inquest. I'm afraid I can't say when that will be. But we will keep you informed at every stage.'

'Do you have any idea who killed him?'

'I'm very sorry, investigations are ongoing at the moment. We will do everything we can to find the perpetrators and ensure due legal process can take place.'

He paused.

'We can offer some support for yourself and your family if you need this? Sergeant Ross here will be happy to arrange that for you?'

'No. We can manage this ourselves. There are things we have to do.'

Josie stood up, crossed her arms again and waited.

'I understand. Sergeant Ross will leave her contact details, so you can call her if you change your mind, or if you remember anything that may be helpful. I'm very sorry that you have been brought such bad news.'

Woodley looked across at Sergeant Ross as the front door closed behind them. The shared glance said 'odd', wordlessly.

....

'So, we want to speak to Jake Harrison – don't know if we'll find out anything about this woman, Jane. Start with Harrison – see if you can get anything on the company first. Who was the Cambridge colleague? Find out anything you can about Birch's routine, who he associated with, whether there are any disciplinary issues. Check up on any financial or legal or criminal history. It's not that likely this was a random ambush, murder and flee from the scene for the sake of robbery. Have we found a laptop? We don't have any cause to search his flat yet, or any other property, so if we can find that laptop before we need to go down that route then it will make things a lot easier. It might be at work. Get that done, and meanwhile see if you can get anything at all on the woman.'

....

'I don't think there's much I can tell you, Sergeant.'

'We're making routine enquiries, Mr Harrison. I understand you worked with Graham?'

'It's a big company. I wouldn't say we were working together all the time.'

'But you did share some work projects, I understand?'

'From time to time.'

'How did you find him? As a colleague?'

'He was a decent bloke. I'd say hardworking - usually stayed late to get things finished.'

'Did you socialise together?'

'Only the very occasional drink at the pub, after work. He didn't like socialising much, I think. Burnt off any stress at the gym.'

'Do you know anything about any relationships he had outside of work?'

'Ha! Can't imagine he had any really. Sorry, that's a bit crass. I just don't think he had the time.'

'His family?'

'Never talked about them, not to me anyway.'

'Did he ever mention someone called Jane?'

'As I said, he didn't talk about his social life. I never heard him mention that name. Where does she come in?'

'We're just making general enquiries, sir. We have to look at everything, however unlikely or irrelevant. Do you know if he was doing any work connected with Cambridge at all, Ipswich, anywhere like that?'

'I can't see how - we're largely south coast based. I'm not aware of any connections he had up there.'

'I take it he would have had a laptop. Do you know anything about that?'

'He had a work laptop, which is still here. We usually hot desk, so desktop computers are only used to connect the laptops to, or we use a docking station. I know he had a personal one too, of course, but I don't remember him using here at all. I imagine he kept it with him.'

'Thank you, we'll check in with your IT department regarding the work computer. Can you remember the last time you saw Graham?'

'It was definitely the Thursday before I understand he was found. He said he had Friday off - I remember, because it was very unusual for him to take extra time off. I left at six - he was still in the office when I left.'

'Was there any chance he had any serious competition or any other issues from other companies, old colleagues, customers, anything like that?'

'Graham was a competitive sort, but only in the sense that he wanted to do the best job, and of course he was sporty - I don't know anything about work issues though. I can't imagine anyone actually being an enemy of Graham. As I said, he was a decent bloke.'

'Thank you for your time, Mr Harrison. Sorry to interrupt your work. It's been very helpful speaking to you.'

....

'So, what do we have?'

'The company is clean, sir, fully registered, up to date with returns, accounts lodged with Companies House and validated. Eventually got hold of Harrison – on the road a lot, defensive and self-important chap, but calmed down when he realised we were determined to get the information we wanted. He said Birch's laptop would have been with him, so I think we might need to do a search of his flat. Work laptop was clean. IT said there would have been any non-business activity flagged. Harrison had no contact with Harrison after Thursday afternoon. Denied any knowledge of bad associations, said Birch was a straightforward sort of person, hardworking. Didn't know anything about a Cambridge contact, said they don't have a branch there or anywhere nearby. Said they didn't socialise much but did meet at the pub occasionally. Hadn't heard him mention anyone called Jane. Birch's social media platforms tallied much with what we already know, no Facebook or Twitter, but he was on LinkedIn, mainly business contacts. No evidence of a Jane in his LinkedIn account, or in work documents – not even a Jane employed by the company, according to HR. Maybe he was going to see her that weekend. By the way, there was some evidence of a passenger having recently been in the car – forensics say it was likely that there would have been something like mud in the footwell on the passenger side, parts of the chassis were preserved from the fire. No chance of fingerprints, DNA, hair, fibres.'

'Don't worry about the possible girlfriend for the moment. An alias, maybe? Husband in the background? Let's get a warrant for the flat. That's the next most obvious place we'll find anything.'

…….

Gloucester South Heights was a new, smart and very expensive block in one of the trendy areas of East London which had once been the bleakest place to live in the city, housing the hand-to-mouth community of the then distinctly working classes. Now, it was upmarket and youthful. The entrance led to a ground floor dedicated to a kind of mall, containing a range of small, nondescript shops providing what seemed to be boutique supplies which were trendy and probably expendable. A reception desk was unmanned, but displayed information providing means of contacting Java Tenorite Superior Housing Solutions. A security guard appeared unobtrusively, and glanced at Bridgeworth's ID.

'We have been notified of your visit, sir.   My colleague will show you to G15 and provide access.'

They passed down a corridor lit with soft, ice blue lighting, into a lift which hummed discreetly, as if to apologise for being something so functional, and reached floor G. From a corridor which was almost entirely pale grey and managed to look and feel luxurious nevertheless, the reached a - grey - door numbered 15.

Flat G15 was white and stone grey, antiseptically clean, and tiny.

'Talk about living like rats in a cage,' said DI Bridgeworth. 'And I bet it cost over half a million. A lovely view over how the other half lives, though. Can see the Thames from here. Open plan kitchen and living area – start in here, Woodley. I'll go and look in the bedroom and the bathroom.'

A compact double bed took up most of the floor space. Fitted cupboards filled one wall, and the shallow shelves housed neatly folded and organised clothing. At the base were two small drawers, containing receipts – for electrical equipment mainly – and a few personal items, letters – mainly advertising circulars – toiletries, magazines, books. He glanced through, seeing only mundane purchases and unremarkable reading matter. There were no notes, letters, anything which identified any personal information. The bathroom was actually a very carefully constructed cupboard, containing a toilet, minute handbasin and shower. There was a small mirror on the wall and a barely functional shelf above the handbasin. Oddly, there was a small, silver plaque just above the mirror, which was engraved with "JTS Housing Solutions: Opportunities for perfect living in a modern world". Not in my world, muttered Bridgeworth.

He felt slightly claustrophobic just trying to turn around after entering the shower room. Everything was white, apart from the black fabric blind over the small window of the bedroom. He took a few moments to look through the drawers and cupboards, checked whether the bed had storage spaces, and looked as best he could underneath.

'Sir! Could you come in here, please?'

'What is it, Woodley?'

'These were under the sofa, sir.'

Wodley presented a crumpled piece of paper, and a row of beads.

'It seems to be an address, maybe, sir.'

'And a necklace?'

'No, it's a rosary, sir – Catholic prayer beads.'

'What's on the paper?'

He took the crumpled note.

'I don't know if it's an address – may be a reminder. What's this … ? "0581 … 7002… 307 … Varovani?" Is that a phone number? Some kind of grid reference, points on a map, maybe? And a person?'

'I don't know, sir. But the occupant of this flat wouldn't seem to be particularly religious – no Bible about, nothing like that. If it was his, he wouldn't keep it under the sofa. Maybe the note's a crossword clue, or something.'

'I have absolutely no idea. Bag them up, Woodley, it's just about all we can take that might be of the remotest use.'

. . . .

'Sir.'

'What is it, Woodley?'

'The Birch case?'

'And?'

'Forensics have just got back on the items. Fingerprints on the rosary are the victim's but also one other's. On the note, the victim's and one other's – but not the same as on the rosary.'

'So – visitors?'

'Who happened to drop their rosary beads under the sofa? But that piece of paper is more interesting.'

'Go on.'

'Nothing clear on the numbers yet – but the word – Varovani?'

'And?'

'It means warning. In Czech.'

CHAPTER FOUR   *'The miserable have no other medicine, only hope.'* (Claudio, *Measure for Measure*)

In an otherwise empty, grimy East End café, three men were in muttered discussion.

'It is getting risky. What do we need to do?'

'If the consignment has been intercepted, then we need to clear up the mess first. Get rid of it all. Get rid of anyone who gets in the way. We have to cut our losses – all of them. And anyone who leaves evidence will go the same way.'

'We have to empty the storage first. It can only go north. Any ports, any sea routes, all will be too risky. It has to be a dead vehicle. Jakub, deal with that. Then we have to empty the houses. That means we can't risk any more leakage. The usual means.'

'We may not need to do that. We can keep control of the houses, for now. It is just unfortunate that we have had the escape. Track down the woman, deal with her, but leave the rest as they are for now. We've cleaned up the traitors. Make sure there aren't any more.'

'What about the police?'

'They're not going to look any further. There isn't enough. Just keep them away from the units. Get the right people to fend them off and get everything moved as quickly as possible. Keep it nice and clean.'

…….

'I think we might need to get OCU in on this, Woodley. I'm not happy that we've got two suspicious deaths, both with maybe tenuous links with organised crime. A warning written in Czech, plus a violent crime, is too much of a coincidence, surely? I need to know what's going on with any trafficking activity now. Get a dossier together, send it over, then we'll set up a meeting.'

…….

DI Matthews of the Organised Crimes Unit was used to being heard.

'We've got a man on the ground, John. We're already working on ops. What you've got doesn't really add anything to what we already know.'

'Which is …?'

'We have a London-based cell which controls at least four operations across the country. This means that there is never a sudden concentration of movement in any of those areas – they spread it around constantly, very clever at covering their tracks. So we have one man in at the centre – he's meant to manage the contacts with the houses. We're thinking of putting a woman in one of the houses, although this means it might be harder to contain activities. There are infiltrators and dissidents all over the place. Usually none of them actually survives. If your two victims are either of these, then I'm afraid they are collateral damage. What we must have is any evidence that can take us directly to the location of the source of operations. We are constantly tracking their digital activity but this is like trying to herd flies. It's too – virtual. In order to break the circle, we need to get to the physical centre of operations. We can add your information, but to be honest it's not really evidence, is it?'
'So, what do you need?'
'We need real names, John. You haven't even got a name for the first victim. And Graham Birch hasn't come up as an alias for any of the known contacts.'
'But you agree there are connections here? '
'No, I don't, John! The first victim could have been anyone. The second may have seen a programme on TV and Googled a word he'd heard and didn't understand. If you could bring me a live witness, then maybe we'd be in business. As it stands, I'm not interested.'
'So what are you getting from your undercover?'
'I can't reveal that informally, as well you know. Except to say that he's getting information which may be useful. But we may have to pull him soon. The gang are getting twitchy, they have had some information leakage and suspect everyone – so if our man gets tied up in that, it could be very messy. We know they're planning to cut and run – but that's more than I should be saying. Forget it John, it's going to be wasted energy.'

…….

'So why are they planning to put in a UCO, if it's getting nasty, sir?'

'This is not a subject for discussion, Woodley. We've got to let that one go. The first victim we can justifiably close, once the paperwork is complete, but the second one is a problem. We've got to carry on a normal investigation there. Anything on the weapon?'

'Nothing more, sir. They have a description of the most likely type of knife, but it would be something that could be bought anywhere, maybe a large pocket knife, or a smallish kitchen knife.'

'Any more witness statements?'

'Nothing. It seems as if he was invisible, from Thursday evening until he was found.'

'Anything from the airport?'

'No arrivals or departures in the name of Birch at any time that week.'

'And no suspects at all?'

'Nothing to implicate anyone who has been identified as a contact.'

'It's a shame we don't have the laptop. As usual, just about everything we need will be on there. No reports of items handed in?'

'Nothing, sir.'

'And nothing on his work computer?'

'All completely legit, sir.'

'Airport CCTV? Flats? Outside work, gym?'

Woodley looked at him. He'd done his share of overtime this week.

'OK, I get the picture. I don't think we can do any more at the moment. Keep both as open cases for now.'

…….

'Excuse me, I'm sorry, everywhere else is taken – do you mind if I sit here?'

'Of course not, please help yourself.' The man smiled.

The woman sat down and stirred her coffee, gazing out of the window. She seemed anxious not to miss something. She glanced at her phone, frequently, and ignored the cooling drink.

'You look as though you're new to the area.'

The woman looked up at the man.

'I'm sorry?'

'Oh, ignore me. You just look as though you're looking for someone – or somewhere?'

'Oh – not really. I'm just – waiting for someone.'

'Of course. I'll shut up. None of my business.'

She smiled back.

'Please, I don't mean to be rude. I'm just going to start a new job. I need to make sure I don't miss them.'

'Oh! Good luck with that – a good job?'

'Housekeeper, I think. I'm not sure.'

The man paused.

'Please, ignore me – I'm being nosey. I hope it all goes well.'

He watched as the woman suddenly left her coffee, and joined a man in the street, who grasped her elbow and hurried her off. He felt it looked wrong – a job she couldn't describe, and a man, rather than a woman, who met her, and rushed her away. It left an uncomfortable feeling, one he was familiar with.

....

She handed in her documents, as requested, for checking. She was taken to a large room, where she joined a group of other women – could this be an interview? She thought she had definitely been given the job. She was sure she had been told the job was waiting for her. Maybe she didn't understand that correctly. She glanced around at the women; they all looked young, under 30. No-one seemed to be prepared to break the ice and speak. The man came back, with a woman.

'Pick up all your belongings, get ready to move. We will take you to the location where you will be working. No, no - you don't need your documents. We will take care of them. You'll get them back later - there are further checks we have to make, with the authorities. Hurry up, the transport is here.'

The young woman paused as she watched the others milling around, unsure. This seemed strange - how many jobs were there? The man appeared at her elbow, nudging her forward.

…….

They had arrived at their destination, after an uncomfortable, smoky journey in an old coach, its windows covered with blinds which could not be adjusted. After the heat of the coach, the cold air hit like a blast of ice. It was dark, and all that could be seen were the lights from a long, low building that looked more like a storage facility, with heavy metal doors and small, high windows. It certainly did not look like any kind of residential or business property. The coach was parked close to the largest door, which was opened by the man who left the coach first. They were hurried quickly out of the coach and through the door. The coach had been parked so close that any attempt to slip out and escape would have been difficult, and in view of the dark and empty surroundings probably foolhardy.

'What is your name?'

'Johanna de Hoek.'

'You will be given a new name – learn it and get used to using it. Do not, ever, speak in your own language. You must speak in English at all times, even to someone from your own country. You will only ever be able to leave the house with myself or Gregor, and only when we require you to do so. You will be given supplies as necessary. You will eat with the other women and will be allowed to sleep in the shared room when you are told – otherwise you will sleep where you work.'

'I don't understand – I thought I would have a job working in the house? And can I have my documents back, and my phone, please?'

'Look, you are here to work, you just need to do as you are told. You don't need your documents. We will take care of them for you.'

The woman left, and Johanna was sure she heard a key being softly turned in the lock.

Johanna looked around her. The room had no windows – she had no idea where she was, after the journey of over an hour. She tried the door, and it was indeed locked – and the other women looked frightened, unfriendly. Flimsy plastic chairs were placed along the walls, a jug of water and paper cups were stood on a small metal table. A door led to a small, grubby restroom. She had been told it will all be good – a permanent job, accommodation. This was not good.

....

Judith was walking along the sea wall. She loved this time, when signs of winter approaching could be sensed, bringing the sharper north-easterly winds across the marsh and stirring the long grass below the wall. She never felt unsafe along this bleak part of the island. She thought of the day she and Gail found the body of that poor man and wondered if the police had identified him. She hoped so – his family would want to know. She kept meaning to get in touch with the police – it was probably nothing, she wouldn't want to be a nuisance. They've got enough to do. But it did keep nagging her.

She had dropped into The Ship – she'd promised to take some tomatoes round, she always had an excess at that time of year, they seemed to take on a final burst – and had got chatting to Geoff. The subject of the body came up, which it tended to do in the weeks after the event, more because it was a mystery rather than because it was a body. Geoff had mentioned someone coming in and asking about it – not a policeman, someone foreign. Said they wondered if they had been identified. Maybe it *was* a relative? But then again, Geoff said he had told them to ask the police. So that put her mind at ease.

…….

Johanna slept fitfully, without rest. The room was hot and airless, even though it was not heated. Others of the women were also restless, some very quietly sobbing, others whispering urgently to their neighbour. Johanna spent every night alternately trying to plan a way out or resigning herself to dying before she could see her family – her home, freedom – again. She tried to occupy herself with getting to know some of the women through observation; in the best moments, she hoped this would help her recognise them in the event of rescue or escape. Sometimes, they would try to speak to compatriots, only to be interrupted by the abrupt arrival of Gregor, somehow knowing they were risking their lives at that moment. On one occasion, he dragged one young girl by her arm from the room, and her cries could be heard for just a few seconds as he pulled her down the corridor. She never returned to the room.

Days passed with no changes to the routine - fitful sleep for a few hours, ended with chunks of stale bread with stale cheese, followed by the anxious tedium of waiting to be half-dragged out of the sleeping quarters to the dark and dirty rooms at the back of the house. The women were offered fixes at some point in the day, instead of food, which Johanna always refused, preferring to be hungry. No-one spoke to them, not even the men, and certainly they didn't speak to each other, for fear of being accused of plotting or lying to the men. Some women refused all food and water, hoping that this would be their way out, but they were always either forced to eat, or dragged away and not seen again. Johanna knew that somehow she had to be stronger, and find a way of escaping, to ensure the women were found and rescued. She was starving, but not poisoned and weakened by drugs, and knew she could find a way, if she kept focused and clear-headed.

She had kept a mental record of the daily activities of Gregor and the woman, who Gregor called Hana. He always went out in the morning at 9.00; the woman went out when he returned, any time from an hour later to several. So there should always be one of them to watch the women. Hana would work in the office while he was away. Johanna could hear her on the telephone, making some arrangements, not loud enough to be able to decipher the words. Then she would leave that side of the house, but presumably was still in the building. Then Gregor would return, check the numbers of women, and line them up for the business of the day. They did not eat until the business was completed, and this was often not until the evening. The food was cheap, sparse, tasteless, tough. She had got used to the hunger, but not the harm she experienced – she was determined, she would never get used to that. But she had to have a plan.

When Gregor returned, the woman would leave. Sometimes she would not return until late in the evening. Gregor could not watch over them that whole time. He had to organise the clients, take money, deal with the ones who felt they had been cheated, or the ones who refused to pay. This was the best time to take a risk – Gregor would have to keep fully focused on what he was doing, to protect himself. If it happened that the other man would be outside, or even better demanding than Gregor go outside with him to fight, then the door, which was kept unlocked for ease of access, could be used for a perilous and very brief escape attempt. She had never seen any of the women try. None of them spoke Dutch, some spoke a little English, but most were too terrified to even try to talk to her. She felt a sense of betrayal, that she might try to leave them. But if she succeeded, then she could get help for them.

One night, Gregor was dealing with a particularly angry and inebriated group of men. He struggled to contain the situation, and she heard him crying out as they beat him. There was no sign or sound of the woman. Johanna slipped quickly and silently through the door, down the corridor, against the wall, until she reached the kitchen door, praying that it would be unlocked – if not, she would shortly be dead. She held her breath and heard the blood pounding in her ears. She breathed again as the door opened. The route was clear, the kitchen door was unlocked, as the women's door alone was strong enough to contain them, if it was properly policed. She ran.
…….

She knew that she was not yet safe. Surrounding the house was moorland; open, flat, cold, exposed. The chill air hit her like a sheet of ice. She shook, from either fear or cold, and the combination of tremor and freezing air snatched her breath. She tried to focus on the surroundings. There was a track leading to the house – she remembered the rough ride in the van. She shouldn't go that way – Gregor would know that would be the obvious route. He would be out instantly, and surely he had backup to help him search for her. The terror came back. Should she hide, or run?

CHAPTER FIVE   *'The robb'd that smiles, steals*
something from the thief.'   (Duke of Venice, *Othello*)

Gregor raged.
The woman standing opposite him bridled.
'So why did you let those men take you outside? It is your stupidity, not mine. The plan was that we would take turns to watch them. Now the gang are going to blame us both, maybe kill us both. You are so stupid – you knew what they would do. Did they find her?'
'Of course they did not find her. They were too busy making it difficult for us. Now the women are useless, too, and there will be no business, and who is going to get the blame for that?'
'What will they do?'

'What do you think they will do, stupid woman? They will kill us all, the women too. They already know about the leak – they might have killed them both, but it's too late to continue as they planned. They will have to start again. It will cost money, and we will be blamed for that.'
'But they need these women to do that. They will move us all, surely.'
'Or just replace us. Don't you think they've got plenty lined up? They'll kill us, they will believe we are too dangerous.'
…….

Johanna had left the house at what must have been around 10.00 p.m., roughly according to the time that seemed to have passed since sunset. The sky was heavily clouded and the moon was low and pale. If it did not rain, then she might be able to find cover to protect her for a few hours, before dawn rose. It took just moments of standing still to think, for her to realise that to find shelter and sleep would be the worst action to take; if she was not found, then she would die of hypothermia. She had no proper clothing, no shoes on her feet, and her physical resources were low. She must keep moving. If she kept herself going forward slowly and steadily, conserving her energy, she could manage to avoid stopping to rest, and would also keep her blood flowing. She would find cover from rain if necessary. She could only hope that a town or village was near – at least she would be able to find somewhere warm to rest there.
Her slow, steady pace served her well, even though she felt herself drift into a state of cold, dark, quiet, endless movement, the sound of her bare feet crunching gently through the dead bracken the only sound to disturb the silence. She had no thoughts as her body continued relentlessly carrying her forward. She felt she had stepped into an endless night. The urge to stop and lie down was overwhelming. Periodically, she would rub her arms and feet, without stopping as best she could.

She had kept the track in sight as well as far as possible, but to one side, at a distance of around 50 metres, knowing that this would be the only chance of reaching a larger road, which must lead to a town of some kind. If she saw a light on the track, she would be far enough away to lie down and stay out of sight. She knew that even in the wildest areas of this country, there would be a town or village within a few miles, and whichever direction she took she would surely reach some signs of life, as long as she avoided doubling back, and finding herself back at the house. Surely, she would be able to reach help. Her bare feet were starting to bleed from contact with the stones in the rough ground, and she was so cold that she had stopped shivering – she just felt a numbness which seemed to warm her. She looked at the sky and could see a lightening creeping over the horizon. At the same time, she was aware of something ahead – not lights, or noise, or smoke – just a sense of life. She arrived at a village after the night of what felt a lifetime carrying herself through the ditches and rough hillocks of the moor.

She approached the village with trepidation. It was early morning, and most of the shops were still closed. She knew she was in a perilous position – her appearance alone would cause suspicion. She was barefoot, unwashed, wearing a thin, cheap, grubby dress, and damp and chilled through from the night on the moor. She was desperate for food and water but knew that to attempt to steal some from the small supermarket would be tremendously risky. She had to find somewhere to think, to try and work out a plan. What if there were people in the village who knew about the house? Would they be involved with it? And would they force her to go back? How would she explain having no money, no car, no clothes? She saw an early morning bakery open which gave some space to a café area, with two small tables and chairs, and a separate counter to sell food and drink. She knew she had no plan, but had to find a way out, and entered the shop with caution.

'Good morning, madam. Can I help you?'

The woman across the counter looked uncertain and seemed to be careful not to stare at the unusual appearance of her customer.

'I am … can you tell me how I can get to the nearest town, please?'

'Are you driving?'

'No – I don't have a car … I'm lost, I think …'

'Where have you come from?'

Johanna tried to laugh apologetically.

'I'm stupid – I decided to go for a walk – got lost on the moor …'

'Goodness … have you been out there all night? Would you like to use our phone, or something?'

'I have no money – I lost my bag …'

'Do you know, I think you ought to call the police, dear – I can do that for you …?'

A woman entered the shop and intervened cheerfully.

'Annie! I've been looking everywhere for you, love! Thank goodness I've found you! Could we have two coffees, please, and some bacon rolls.' She handed over a note and smiled with brisk confidence at the shopkeeper, who bustled off, glad to be relieved of an unwanted responsibility.

Hana had found her. Johanna slumped in the chair, tears aching behind her eyes.

'I want you to listen to me and not say a word.'

Johanna could not look at the woman. She couldn't bear to cry; she was too overwhelmed and exhausted, knowing now that the suffering had to continue even further.

'You must listen to me. I have a contact. He will be here in under three hours. His name will be given as Kyle. He will pick you up and take you to London. I have agreed with a woman in the village that she will hide you until she receives a message that he has arrived, but then you must leave her house and meet Kyle at the end of School Lane. It is essential that no connection with this woman is made. You must never mention her. If she gives you a name, it will not be her real one. Kyle will take you to London and you will be safe.'

Johanna could not speak. She didn't understand. Was she being taken to the gang who took her?

'I would rather die here than go back ...'

'No. You must understand. I work for the police. No-one must know we have met; all anyone knows is I have come to the village for supplies. This is the woman's address. It is near – just cross the road, walk down the road that way, and take the lane on the left, just after the butcher's. You must go there straight away. I will speak to the owner here in the shop and explain that she must not say either of us have been here. I can only tell you to do this, and if you don't you will definitely be killed. Your name now is Jane Kingston. Remember it. I've got to get bread and take it back. I can't be here any longer.'

Johanna felt she would cry, but nothing came. She had drunk half her coffee and had two bites of the roll. She left the shop and walked, barefoot, to the woman's house.
…….
The woman in the village ushered her quickly through the door.
'You know I can't do anything other than give you some supplies and let you rest until the transport arrives. This address must never be revealed to anyone.'
'I understand. I'm very grateful …'
'Just get yourself out of this country and back home, love.'
The woman gave her clean clothes, trainers and cash, and let her rest in one of the bedrooms. When the woman received the message, Johanna was in an exhausted and restless sleep.
'Jane! Jane!'
The woman's voice mixed with her turbulent dreams. She awoke in panic, waiting to be dragged from the bed.
'Quick! You must go immediately! Here, I've put everything in a bag.'
Johanna, now Jane, pulled her scattered thoughts together and tried to grasp the situation. The woman took her to the back door, gave her quick verbal directions, and closed the door quickly behind her.
Jane walked down the narrow path, to a gate set into a wall at the end of the garden. Her heart was pounding with sudden waking and the mix of fear and hope. She knew there were some 200 metres of walking ahead of her, to get to the end of the alleyway at the back of the houses and then to the dead end of a rough, single lane street.
She hurried forward, head down, until she could see the small grey car with smoked windows at the end of the road. A man leaned out and pulled in her bag.
'Get in, quick. Don't speak.'

The man had spun and accelerated away sharply before she had had time to put on her seat belt. He didn't slow until he had reached a straight, empty stretch of road away from the village. She glanced briefly at his face – he didn't look like someone who would be involved with the people running the houses. He looked – ordinary. She glanced away. This was not the time to trust anyone.

He had not spoken to Jane or looked at her, until they were at a steady speed along the open road. Either side were flat stretches of greyish brown moorland, dipping and concealing, scattered with sheep and ponies. Jane felt exhausted and powerless.

The man turned to glance at her.

'Please don't worry. Come on, drink, eat – it's all in the bag. You can call me Kyle. I'm going to take you to a safe house. I'm not in the police, but I am a friend. Once I drop you off, you must go straight in, knock at the door and say you have been brought there by a friend. Don't mention any names, at all. Except your own - Jane. We can't stop on the way, I'm afraid. You'll get proper food when you're there. Once we're on the motorway, we should be safer, but it's not worth the risk of being seen.'

Jane gazed out of the window. She couldn't speak.

The man slowed a little, and looked at her briefly, more closely.

'I'm sure I know you.'

'No, you don't know me.'

Jane had seen too many men in recent weeks to care. She didn't want to be recognised.

'The café – in London. You came in, said you had a new job …. I could have said something …'

Jane looked at him, relieved for some reason she didn't understand. It was as if she was back there, before all this happened. It felt like a different world - she had been a different person. Still, she couldn't speak. She remembered him now, though by his voice, rather than his face. He had sounded kind then.

'I'm sorry – I'm really sorry I didn't stop you. I can't really tell you anything. But I can get you to safety.'
Jane was desperate for sleep. She looked away, to the fat little ponies grazing slowly and pensively on the scrub, oblivious to the complexities of the human world.
…….
Jane slept. She was clean, warm, fed. A woman called Grace had given her what she needed, saw her bedded down and left her. Jane had realised that she didn't know the name of the woman in the shop, the woman in the cottage. But here was Grace, almost ironically, her saviour. She needed to return home.
…….
'We have cleansed the house.'
The men were seated around a grubby packing box in a locked, empty warehouse. The air was heavy with sickly sweet smoke, and the floor was grimy with accumulated grease.
'So, what now?'
'What's happening with the goods, Jakub?'
'It's sorted. We have got the supply lines in place. The consignment will be cleaned up. We have to prepare for the next one. We have organised a group of carriers, coming in by air, and pickups are agreed.'
'Where?'
'Everywhere. The handovers will be – sorted.'
'Get me a list of the handover points. I want to make sure they're dealt with.'
'What about the leaks?'
'The woman has gone, disappeared. We have dealt with the house. We know there was an undercover involved. They've all been eliminated. We don't know what's already been passed on.'
'Can we get the woman?'
'We lost all the passports in the fire. If she got away with help, then she'll have a new identity.'
'What are we going to do?'

'We can try to track her. We know where the women came from. If it's not too late, we can get to the borders. But if it is too late, then we've got to carry on getting all new stock in place, clearing out the wasters. No mercy. Everything - everyone - goes, that might pick up the trail. Get on it.'

....

Jane glanced at the passport. She looked at the reflection of the new version of herself, with short, brown hair, simple but expensive jeans, tee shirt and trainers. Johanna – and Jane – were gone, apparently. She must remember, she is Kate Harman. Katherine.

Kyle was waiting, in a different car. Jane had wanted to leave a gift for the women, but nothing seemed anything but ridiculous. They didn't need gifts, just money. When she returned to Amsterdam, she would arrange something, somehow. She wouldn't care if her new identity was compromised. She wasn't going to let anyone dictate to her anymore.

The airport felt mundane, loud, real, human. It was as if she had woken from a nightmare and become a normal person again. She had to keep to the plan for a short while longer.

'Would passengers travelling on flight number 382 to Amsterdam please proceed to Gate 7, as boarding has commenced. Please have your passports and boarding passes ready for checking. Have a pleasant flight and thank you for flying with us on KLM. Last call for flight number 382 now boarding, for Amsterdam …'.

CHAPTER SIX   *'Speak less than thou knowest.'*   (The Fool, *King Lear*)

DI Matthews sat for some time, looking at his desk, seeing nothing, his hand resting against his face. This would take some explaining. Meanwhile, he had to break the news.

'Harris, things have not gone to plan.'

'Sir?'

'I'm afraid we've lost DC Kemble.'

Harris paused – he knew it wasn't a good idea to state the obvious or, worse, make the wrong assumption.

'The house was taken. One of the women managed to escape. It was inevitable that she would talk, and they couldn't get her back before she was got by a rescue group. The house was locked with all its occupants inside, set alight.'

'Caroline …?'

'Everyone died. We found Kemble. There were nine other female bodies, and one male. We assume that was Gregor Rusu. He has been on our watch list for some time, he was known as a key organiser for the houses. Kemble was able to pass on a lot of useful intel, and we can't discount that. I would imagine she also arranged the rescue, but couldn't pass on any contact information before the OCG got to her.'

'I'm sorry, sir.'

'I'll deal with it. I don't want you taking on the family. It's my responsibility here. We have to take what we can from this. We'll have a meeting, once the team have taken it on board. Take a break if you want, Harris.'

'I'm OK sir. Do you want me to speak to the team?'

'No, I'll do that now.'

…….

'This has been an unfortunate event, and we recognise that it is a tragedy, for a very promising young officer, and for her family. But we also have to look at where it leaves us. We're going to have to redouble our efforts, as the gang will now be regrouping and making plans. Thanks to DC Kemble, we know that they have now moved physical goods – including the women they have left – up north, kept some ops down south, presumably to try and contain the number of people involved. We have to identify all names as far as we can, strengthen port surveillance, track down any locations, speak to contacts. What's this rescue faction which seems to be involved?'

'A group calling themselves Action Against Slavery, sir. No formal online presence, as far as we can find out. Seems to be word of mouth, or through personal comms. So probably quite a small group, but with access to at least one safe house, contact with authorities, mobility, organisation of fake IDs. We are looking at DC Kemble's computer records and phone at the moment, looking for any possible links.'

'OK, keep on it. Let me know immediately if we have anything we can use. Names?'

'We have Jakub Rusu – Gregor's brother – and Andrei Vulpe. We know that they have used buildings owned by Frank Beckswith, in London, but we can't track him down yet. He ran a used car business in Stepney apparently, seems to have closed that down. They are tight though, sir. If they use anyone for transport, accommodation, that sort of thing, they do so under cover of alternate business – usually manage to create what seem to be legit documents. With aliases, of course. All have fake passports, presumably, as we know they travel to Europe, but have not come up on any database.'

'Locations?'

'They move all the time, sir. They use somewhere once, then leave. Too clever normally to do anything drastic to get rid of any evidence. But it's just about impossible to track them, let alone get any forensics.'

'Any more evidence of victims?'

'Most are likely to be unknown contacts. They don't tend to keep records of who they have dealings with, or at least we've never been aware of any. The assumption is they get rid of anyone who causes problems.'

'How does that sit with reports of missing persons?'

"Most are from Europe, sir. There's a sort of no man's land, where once the individuals leave Europe and are taken by the OCG, it becomes impossible to trace them, simply because all personal evidence is destroyed. And bodies are disposed of very efficiently it seems, so any chance of getting DNA is practically nil.'

'Any knowledge of informers?'

'There must be some way that the AAS group get information about the activities. It's more likely that DC Kemble contacted them, than the other way round – we've got no record of contact from them. At the moment, the only obvious route would be from an insider, out. But without more knowledge of their movements and organisation, we can't do much.'

'Which is why we had DC Kemble on the inside. It is crucial that we find out as much as we can about her connections. I would guess that she would not be able to feed back to us until it was a done deal – if there was any chance of any kind of police presence, then the risk would be increased tenfold. Can you investigate the AAS group, Harris?'

'On to it, sir.'

……..

'We're not worrying about making arrests, anything like that, at this point – we'd just like to know whether you have any concerns about anyone who uses the centre – anyone at obvious risk, for example?'

DS Harris was seated at a folding metal table with a young man, who appeared incongruous with his dreadlocks and smartly labelled – 'Respite and Recovery' – and official blue polo shirt. The room appeared chaotic, with men and women of all ages variously seated in corners, on chairs or the floor, or gathering slowly around a long trestle table, where hot food was being served from large tureens. The atmosphere was well organised and good-humoured. Some of the attenders were cowered and defensive, but all were fed and accepted without discrimination.

'Ha! Everyone here is at risk, officer. It's not just the young ones, who might have drugs, or money, and are vulnerable to assaults. The older ones, weakened with drugs or alcohol or just exposure, we see them come in every day, with wounds, black eyes, bruises – or worse, we find them on the streets, too late. Don't ask me why some people like to spend their time beating up people who are unlucky enough to find themselves in bad circumstances. There you go. We feed them, give them somewhere warm for a bit, provide some basic medical attention, have a chat if they want – but we don't have the resources to give them somewhere to shower, or sleep, or brush their teeth. We try and work with other organisations to get people passed on to somewhere more permanent, but it's not as easy as that. People become conditioned to their circumstances, lose all confidence and self-esteem. They believe the labels other people put on them.'

'I realise it's difficult. At least you're doing something. I'm mainly interested in whether you have contact with anyone who may be in a situation where they may be under coercion of some kind?'

'If you're asking about illegal immigrants, I can't help you there. Simply because we don't know. We don't ask questions of anyone who comes in.'

'I hear what you're saying. But if someone is a victim of crime, it is our business. We're not looking for people who have voluntarily entered the country illegally. We're looking for anyone who may have been forced into a situation against their will.'

'That's hard to judge. People don't open up to us too readily. Their trust has been abused already. But there's a group down on Hamblin Street, somewhere called Mary House. It's a women's group, they tend to provide resources to women who are abuse victims, but they support any woman who is vulnerable. They might be prepared to help.'

'Thanks. Have you heard of group called Action Against Slavery, by the way?'

'You name it, there's a group called it somewhere. They tend to be short-lived and misguided. I haven't heard of them, but I don't take any notice of factions or protest groups. It all tends to be a bit pointless in the end. I don't see any of them genuinely changing people's lives for the better. Money, homes, jobs – that's all that's needed. Could you excuse me, I really need to give a hand? It's getting late, so it's getting busy.'

'Of course. Thank you for your time.'

…….

The house took some time to find. A small plaque next to the door was plain and just showed the name of the building. The woman who answered the door, after checking his identity, lifted the chain and stood back to let him in. She showed him into a small room and leaned forward on the desk between them.

'So, what can I do for you, officer?'

'I'm just making some enquiries, Mrs …?'

'I'm Alice. What are you making enquiries into?'

'Alice. We're looking into a possible situation of coercive abuse. I'd just like to see if you can provide us with any information, anything you might have come across, heard about …?'

'Is it a specific case?'

'At the moment we are just investigating whether we can find any evidence of such cases.'

'That sounds very vague. I would have thought you must have a reason.'

'We're just making enquiries. Is there anything you could tell us that may be helpful?'

'The women – and girls – who come here are almost always desperate, officer. We will advise them of sources of practical support and make calls for them if necessary. We are not a refuge as such, so can't offer anything like proper accommodation, it would be too risky for all involved. But we can give them some immediate help, some basic medical treatment if necessary, a couple of nights basic respite at best, and put them in touch with the right people.'

'What do you do for them?'

'Mainly that. But we can offer a short-term rescue situation. For example, if a woman is at immediate risk. We have a reasonable degree of security. You'll have noticed the camera at the door – there are several throughout the building. No-one is allowed to open the door except myself, or Grace if I'm not here. We both live on site. Obviously, men are not usually admitted – of course, I understand we must make an exception for the police. But even then, we have to be careful. Sometimes anonymity is preferable to investigation.'

'I can see why that might be the case. Have you got any particular concerns about any of the women?'

'I had a girl come in a month or so ago, said she knew where women were being held against their will. I suggested she go straight to the police – I never saw her again. She seemed well dressed, spoke perfect English, I didn't have concerns at the time. Then there was a woman a week or so ago, was dropped off by a man I think, she said he was a friend. She said she had been told she must stay indoors for two days, until she was picked up again. Sometimes we have a brief call to let us know that someone is coming in, but not in this case. I couldn't get any more from her. She gave me £50 to keep her here for 48 hours. We don't take payment, but she said she had been told we must take it. Later that day she received a parcel – I'm afraid we have to check everything, it's a condition of our acceptance of anyone. It contained new clothes, shoes, toiletries. I did try to persuade her to speak to the police, if she was at risk, but she was insistent. She was well spoken, had a slight accent, European, I think. Looked as if she may have been living rough for a while, although she was neatly dressed. As much as we want women to be safe, we can't force anyone to take any action, unless we have immediate concerns for someone's safety, and believe they are not able to speak for themselves, or are injured. We have no authority beyond that of any individual who has the right to call emergency services. So we could only see her go, a couple of days later. She didn't seem distressed, just anxious.'
'Did she tell you anything about where she had been?'

'As I said, she refused. She was polite and appreciative, but stayed in the small partitioned dormitory – we can accommodate four women at a time – or the lounge, reading. She did ask if we had a Bible – we have one available, and a Koran. We have a Catholic priest who has agreed to make himself available if any of the women wish to take confession. But we can't provide for any specific needs. Not that we get many requests for spiritual input. And we don't encourage religious gatherings in the house. Generally, women want a safe space, food, shower and a bed.'

'Did she go out, at all?'

'The women here are not prisoners – they are free to leave if they wish, but we don't encourage casual trips outside. To be honest, most women are reluctant to venture out of the house, because of the risk to themselves. They know it is likely they are being looked for.'

'Is there anything else which you've remembered, or thought odd?'

'I don't let myself think of anything as odd. We can't allow ourselves to care too much for these women. We will listen if they wish to talk, but that rarely happens. I'm afraid many eventually just go back to the situations they came from.'

'Well, if you do remember anything that might be of interest to us, do let us know. I'll leave my card here.'

CHAPTER SEVEN   *'Time shall unfold what plighted cunning hides.'*   (Cordelia, *King Lear*)

'How are things in CID, DS Woodley?'

'Hello mate – just passing?'

'You could say that. Look, we've got something interesting. Matthews isn't going to take this up – you know what he's like – his case is his case. But I just want to run something by you, unofficially.'

'Unofficially always sounds good to me. Something you're on?'

'We're trying to track down an OCG, small but big, if you know what I mean. Trafficking mainly – people and drugs. You know we lost DS Kemble?'

'Of course. That's bad, I'm sorry. What happened?'

'Look, in my view it was a complete mess-up. This is unofficial?'

'Unofficial.'

'She shouldn't have gone in. It was too remote, Gregor Rusu was a timebomb, out of control. Everything was managed from outside. He died in the fire, by the way – we don't know about his brother, or Vulpe. They're all we can name at the moment. One of the women escaped. I know you've been looking into two deaths, one a confirmed murder, the other a possible. What can you tell me? Unofficially.'

'First one, probably an Eastern European, cause of death uncertain. Some suspicious injuries and a tattoo, authorities refuse to confirm he would definitely be a link with anything, trying to make out he was just a hustler, went too far somehow. The other death a murder by person or persons unknown. Seems clean, but his laptop hasn't been found. But we found one interesting item in his flat – a crumpled note, with the word *varovani* on it. A warning, in Czech, apparently. And the man from the coast had the word *svoboda* tattooed on his arm – freedom, again in Czech. Doesn't Matthews know all this?'

'If he does, he's keeping it close to his chest. I'm guessing he doesn't want to risk anyone taking his glory. Look, can we just keep this on the simmer for a bit? I don't want to let it go, but I know if I take it to Matthews he'll suppress it.'

'OK, but be careful. If we have to wrap them both up, then we've lost the lot. By the way, what were the names you mentioned, the gang members?'

'Gregor and Jakub Rusu, and Andrei Vulpe.'

'Look, hang on … isn't Vulpe the name for a fox or something?'

He picked up his phone.

'Yep, genus Vulpes.'

'And …?'

The man on the beach had what looked like a wolf's head tattooed on his back.'

'OK. So …'

'A fox's head could look like a wolf's head?'

'Look, we need to get together and go through this. If you're free tonight, hang on for a bit?'

…….

'So … we've got Island Man and Birch for CID, and we've got the Rusus and Vulpe for OCU. Let's just go over what we have for each of them, then see what we've got.'

'Island Man … no identifying evidence. Old injuries to face, no internal injuries. Pathology bit cautious on that, owing to effect of submersion over maybe a few days, usual stuff. Dead before he entered the water, so he didn't drown. Dressed in outdoor type clothes, no shoes or boots. Third and fourth fingers missing on his right hand. Two incisors missing. Wolf's head – or fox's head? – tattoo to right upper back over scapula. Tattoo along left forearm, the word s*voboda*, Czech, could mean either 'freedom', or a surname. Probably Eastern European. Wearing a shoulder strap attached to an empty belt pouch, no fastening, no contents. No DNA records, no fingerprint records, no dental records, no passport. No identification on him.

'Intel via Prague police – wolf's head tattoo is associated with reactionary groups, opposing the gangs, and a common form of punishment amongst the traffickers themselves is to remove the third and fourth fingers of the dominant hand. But both may be coincidental.'

'And Birch?'

'Identified by driving licence. 32, UK resident, white British. Systems analyst, nothing of suspicion related to work. Body found by side of A120 early hours of the 9th, car found burnt out about quarter of a mile away. Death as a result of four stab wounds to the chest and neck, no weapon found. Cash and cards not taken, but as I said, laptop has not been found. Car too damaged to look for fingerprints or any other evidence. No contact with work or family since Thursday evening. Work colleague, Jake Harrison, nothing there. Family mentioned a Jane, couldn't be identified as linked with Birch. Items found at his flat – a rosary, which seems to have fallen under the sofa, and the crumpled piece of paper, containing a set of numbers and a word, *varovani*, Czech for warning.'

'Right, so OCU. We have a small but insidious group of traffickers, with three members known. Andrei Vulpe seems to be the leader. There are – were – two brothers, Gregor and Jakub Rusu. Gregor died in a fire at one of the properties they used to contain women they had trafficked for prostitution. The fire occurred after one of the women escaped. Unfortunately, as you know, one of our DSs was undercover, and died in the fire. The woman who escaped seems to have had help from an organised rescue body. There's a group called Action Against Slavery, who may be involved, or may not. We have reason to believe at the moment that DS Kemble had connections with this group. All the passports held by the women and all documents were destroyed in the fire. We know that the gang are ruthless in eliminating anyone who presents a risk of exposure. Presumably they instigated the fire and have been on the track of the escaped woman. They have used a chap in London, Frank Beckswith, who's been involved with supplies. Can't find him, of course.'

'So, what's ongoing?'

'Mainly trying to track the supply chain. Consignments coming in are sent down a fairly complicated route so that there are a number of intermediaries who are involved in the transit of unidentified goods. They tend to be dealt with if they get suspicious. The movement of the women usually is down an initially legitimate path.   Typically, the women respond to adverts in the posts of respectable companies, offering good pay and opportunities for women with specific skills – administration, PA, nursing, housekeeping, childcare. That's level one. They're provided with free travel to Britain by appropriate and legitimate routes – level two. They're met at the airport and taken to a hotel room, treated well, gifted a welcome package and basically lulled into a false sense of security – level three. A pleasant and professional woman explains that their passports are needed for checking with immigration. Level four, and the turning point. The women are then told they will be taken to their respective jobs and will be given a lift by coach. In fact, they are not taken to any jobs, but to their final destination, which will normally be a house or lockup in a relatively remote location. The windows of the coach will have fixed blinds, of course. They are locked in, have no access to communications, receive very basic food and water and are paid with crack cocaine and heroin. Unless there is an intervention, they probably won't leave, and will usually become addicts, used by customers and abused by the guards.

'So – we're trying to find the first point of exchange of goods – and the location of properties. We know that ops are moving up north and we just want to get to that point where the plans are made. We need to identify carriers, drivers, legitimate contacts. We're making some progress with the borders, in that an initiative is ongoing to identify transit routes – if a woman enters the country having come indirectly from any of the Eastern European countries via any of the known transit points, then they are flagged and we can look into documentation, evidence of communications and so on. But that has to be done immediately on arrival, because if it's not then they're lost. We're having some success with that already. A number of women have been encouraged to return home for various reasons – usually told that there are problems with their work visa or passport. We can't risk identifying the real reason at that point. But to be honest, the number we do manage to catch are the tip of the iceberg.'

'What about this group, Action Against Slavery?'

'I'm trying to make contact. They're not very professional, if I can call it that. Not organised. Too many idealists, a few risk takers. They seem to think that involvement by the police will rock the boat.'

'I suppose they may well be right, considering what happened to Caroline. What are we going to do with all this?'

'Look, I'll let you know if I get any further with this group. Sorry mate, but I think the onus is on you to get something on those two deaths, sharpish. It's the only way we'll move this forward, before we lose the chance.'

'I'll speak with the boss. He won't be happy. Frustrated he can't get Matthews on side; feels he's not doing his job. I'll see if I can get him to let me make some more enquiries.'

'Such as?'

'I want to know who Jane is.'

…….

John Bridgeworth prided himself on his level-headed, pragmatic and professional approach. He used it whenever he felt he was either being undermined or taken for a fool. Sometimes it could be a little more difficult to summon. DCI Hammond didn't make it easy.

'Our job is to find out why and how people are victims. That's it. We're after conviction, as simple as that. Have you got any suspects?'

'Well, no, sir, but …'

'So how are we going to get them?'

'That's what I'm trying to do, sir.'

'No, it's not. You're getting involved in OCU. Not only is it not your job, it's dangerous and it's foolhardy. These are two separate cases. There is no hard evidence that the man on the coast was a victim of crime. Circumstantial factors, not even evidence. If he was murdered, how do you propose to find the pathway? If there is anything to go on, it's more likely to link to organised crime, isn't it? Sometimes we have to just accept that an individual is not part of society, it's as simple as that. It's life. The second one, start looking at known felons, do the usual job of working through all cases with this MO where they're not still in prison. Means and opportunity will do. Plenty of them don't need a motive. Get me a file together and let's find some genuine suspects.'

'Sir.'

…….

'Where can I meet you?'

'We will communicate only by these two phones. Remember, there is no payment without the goods.'

'So how will the payment take place?'

'You give us the information first. When it checks out, you'll get payment.'

'Not good enough. I want some proof.'

'Then you take the risk or give up the chance. If we don't get the information, then your life won't be worth anything anyway, will it?'

'I want in. That's the only way you'll get what you want. You know what I can offer. You need me.'

'Then you'd better have something worth having, or you will find you end up with nothing. You will be nothing.'

'So how do I get in?'

'You wait.'

The man standing in the abandoned car lot looked at his phone for a few moments, then up at the grey and rumbling sky. It begins.

CHAPTER EIGHT   ' 'Tis best to weigh the enemy more mighty than he seems.' (Lewis the Dauphin, *Henry V*)

Autumn was undeniably well under way.

The sea had that touchy air, when it seemed to irritate the shore, rather than caress it. Judith smiled. She couldn't help regarding the sea as organic. The sea was that eternal paradox. Beautiful, calming, melodic. But also savage, cold, ruthless. And she wouldn't have it any other way. It reminded us, she felt, that we must respect nature, as well as love it.

She brushed her hair from her face, as the wind was building, gusting in surreptitiously and low from the sea. She glanced across the shoreline, the memory of the discovery of the body creeping back. She felt a sense of powerlessness, annoyance that her relationship with the sea had tarnished a little.

It was getting cold. She pulled her coat around her and decided to get in and spend the evening with a good film and a half bottle of wine. As she entered her kitchen, she was pulled up short. The leaflet glared at her from the pinboard. She had agreed to host the quiz night at The Ship. The teacher in her metaphorically gritted her teeth, abandoned her plans and got on with it. The coat came on again.

…….

'About time then! Thought you weren't coming!'

'Really? As if I would abandon you all! I've got the paperwork – give me a minute and we'll start the evening.'

She smiled at Geoff over the counter as she ordered a drink.

'Everything OK, Geoff? Been busy?'

'All good. Back to normal for a while.'

The islanders had the usual love/hate relationship with their summer visitors. They brought custom and money, and many of them were happy and well-behaved souls, but the combination of free time, sunshine and alcohol brought the usual challenges.

'Had that chap in again earlier this week.'

'Sorry?'

'The chap I mentioned. Asking about the dead body.'
'But I thought he went to the police?'
'I told him to do that. Whether he did or not, who knows.'
'What did he want this time?'
'Asked if the police had been round. I said I hadn't seen anything since then.'
'What was he like?'
'Middle aged, I suppose. Bit heavy built. Not the usual type we get here.'
'What do you mean?'
'Gruff, not interested in small talk.'
A man called from the tables.
'I'm on it, Jim. I'll be there in a second.'
She turned back to Geoff.
'I'll catch up later. Cheers.'
Judith found the thought of the man didn't shift, after she had left the pub and started to return home. She remembered Jack, and his dramatic pronouncements of impending massacre. Her cottage was not far from the pub, but at the end of an unmade lane which narrowed from the tarmacked road outside The Ship. It was near closing time, and the lane was quiet, as few would be travelling in this direction – they would be going the other way along the road, up to the denser residential areas. She never usually felt vulnerable, walking this way from the pub. What if that man was murdered on the island, and thrown out to sea? Who murdered him? Were they still on the island? She hadn't heard if the police had got anyone yet. She reached her door, turned the key and told herself to get a grip.
The next morning, she rose with the memory of the evening in the forefront of her mind. She felt vaguely that maybe she should have contacted the police, after first hearing that someone had enquired. She reassured herself that her call would probably have been received with dismissal. But this time …
The woman at the end of the line was brisk.

'Do you have a crime number?"
'No, I just wanted to speak to the officer who came to Myres Island …'
'Do you know the name of the officer?'
'No, he came asking some questions …?'
'What date was this, please?'
'Oh, it was early September …'
'And what was it in connection with?'
Judith decided she might as well be brisk, too.
'The body found on the beach on Myres Island.'
'Ah yes.'
The woman seemed relieved to have a focal point.
'That would be DS Woodley. I'll see if he's available.'
There was a silent pause.
'DS Woodley.'
'Oh! Good morning, Sergeant. This is Judith Pendleton. It's in connection with the discovery of the body on the beach here on the island.'
'Of course, I remember. How can I help you?'
'A few weeks ago, the landlord at the pub mentioned to me that a man had been enquiring about the incident. And he's been back.'
'I see. Can you tell me any more about it?'
'Not really. Geoff said he was middle aged, a gruff type. Asked if the police had been to the island.'
'Did the man give a name? Or mention any names?'
'I'm fairly sure he didn't. Shall I ask the landlord to give you a call?'
'I don't think it's necessary at the moment, Mrs Pendleton. I'll make a note of it. Is your phone number the same?'
'It is.'
'Then, if you don't mind, I'll give you a call if I need to ask anything more?'
'Of course. Thank you, Sergeant.'
'Thank you, Mrs Pendleton, for taking the time to let us know.'

Judith put down the phone quietly. She knew the Sergeant wouldn't call back. The world seemed to have shifted very slightly.

....

A man and a woman were seated by the side of the river, in animated conversation. The light and warmth of the summer morning, after a particularly brutal winter and a cold spring, drew out crowds of people, visitors and residents, taking the opportunity to relax in the growing sunshine, enjoy the shade of the lush trees along the banks, watch the bridges and the river come to life, even risk taking off a jacket and feeling the sun on skin. The couple didn't seem to be doing the same.

'I'm not sure, Jo. There will be another job. I can help out, until you get something. You hear about all sorts of risks.'

'I have checked it all out, Jan. It was a legitimate agency. They will find me a job which exactly matches what I'm looking for, provide all transport, deal with the immigration side, even visas. They guarantee at least a year's work, in Britain, very good pay – then I can come back, and we can sort out the family debts, finally. I can't afford not to be working. And a year or so in Britain will be good experience.'

'You must keep in contact, all the time. I don't want to go back to Amsterdam and leave you here.'

'Go back, and don't worry. I will phone you, as soon as I land, and then once I'm settled. I have to go, there is a pickup to the airport. Are you sure you will be able to get back OK?'

'That is the least of my concerns, JoJo. I have my phone; you must phone as soon as you are in London.'

The two parted, but nothing changed on the banks of the Vltava.

....

Jan could not decide which would be the wisest move. If he stayed here in Prague, then he may not be in contact with any communications to the family in Amsterdam from Johanna. But this was where she left. It was two days now, and he had not heard from her. He tried, without hope, to call again, and again, but still the number was unavailable. But then, maybe he needed to chase up the contacts in Amsterdam. She said that she had been to an agency – should he be looking for that? He could not let their parents know, not just yet, and if he returned, then they would obviously ask about Jo. He could not tell them, not just yet.

He came back down to the river, his practised eye watching for the tell-tale signs of the pickpockets and thieves, themselves scanning the crowds with their ill-protected possessions, occupied with the views and the entertainments. So surely, there must be connections here? Maybe the agency is innocent and would not be able to help. Who could he find to speak to here? Could he go to the police? What would they do? Would that put Jo at risk? He couldn't stay in Prague much longer; he needed to get back to Amsterdam.

He bought a *kielbasa* and a beer from a street seller, and sat on the bench they had shared, before they parted. He would go to the police. He had to. They may dismiss him, send him back to Amsterdam to make enquiries there, but he could not allow himself not to at least try. They might be able to direct him to the agency. He wished he had asked Jo for full details. He dropped the half-eaten breakfast into a bin and went to look for the police station.

....

The police officer was polite, but brusque.

'We can't really do much from our side, sir. Your sister is a Dutch national. You need to go back to Amsterdam and register her as a missing person with the police there.'

'But surely you must have some dealings with situations here, people who are known to be involved in things like this? Kidnapping?'

'I understand you are anxious, sir. But all you have to go on is that fact that you cannot reach your sister by phone, and she has not called you. People do lose their phones. You need to go back to Amsterdam, get some details about the agency, get them to look into it. They must have information about your sister's whereabouts and can contact her for you. I assure you, sir, in 99% of cases where people go offline for a bit, it's due to carelessness. Go back to Amsterdam – if they need to contact us, then they will.'

....

He needed to find out when he could get a flight to Amsterdam. He had to get back, if only because he couldn't see what he could do in Prague, other than seek out criminals, which would probably end badly. As he hurried away from the police station, lost in thoughts and plans, after a while he realised he was in an unfamiliar part of the city. He knew much of the city well, having worked there for a number of years, but knew that there are always parts of our most known environment, however long we have lived there, which come as a surprise if we discover them. But this felt different. He knew he was away from the Old Town, but was not in the more mundane business or shopping areas. And he couldn't orient himself to the river. Confused by his uncertainty, he was unaware of the young man crouching in the doorway of a long-closed cobbler's shop. He didn't see the knife until the dark corner of the doorway gave way to sunlight as he walked past, and the glint flared like a small, silent explosion from a gun. Jan raised his arms to protect himself, turning shoulder on to the boy. The knife grazed his arm but missed its mark, and Jan had time to hook a foot behind one of the boy's ankles, causing him to fall backwards on to the stone step of the doorway. The boy lay still on the floor, blood pooling slowly around his head. Shock flooded Jan's body with adrenalin and then numbness, as he felt himself slip helpless to the floor. He started to breathe again, as he felt nausea overtake him. The boy was still motionless. Jan knew he should help but couldn't bring himself to touch the boy. He tried to focus. He could summon help if he ran to an area where there were shops, offices maybe. Desperation to get away threw him forward, away from the boy. After running for some 20 metres, he turned to glance at the boy again. He was moving, trying to raise himself on an elbow. Glad that he was alive, and glad that he, Jan, was not there with him, he ran, revived, to the corner of the street, where he paused to think through the next step. He couldn't just

leap on anyone, ask them to help, then run away. He couldn't use his phone. But he trusted to confusion, went into a large and busy grocery store, and said that someone had been attacked in the street. As people gathered round, he left. As he walked away, he held his jacket sleeve against his arm to try and pack the flow of blood.
....
It was too late to book on to a flight. He had no more towels to stem the bleeding. It must be deeper than he thought. It was getting late, and shops were closing. He could get to the city health centre, but a stab wound always raised suspicions, and led to questions. He felt faint with the effort of thinking. He would have to leave the guest house – he would leave cash to cover the cost. Luckily, he had been careful to prevent signs of his injury, although he would have to steal the towels, and discard them. He knew there was a boat, permanently moored under one of the bridges, which provided a night's accommodation, for a voluntary fee, for the city's homeless. If he went there, he could at least wait until the morning, when he could get to the airport. He could not remember which bridge, but he had to find it. Surely it would be the only hope, as they must witness crimes all the time. They wouldn't have the resources to report them all.

He was met by a man who said his name was Matyas. 'We can dress that wound for you, but it is your responsibility to seek treatment. We can give you a bunk for tonight. You will be woken at six and will be on your way. The rules are strict. Any fighting, any threats, any bad language, any alcohol or drugs, and you'll be out, whatever the time. We can give you a meal now, then you must bunk down and keep out of trouble. If you need any help with legal advice, if you are escaping violence, we can help you find that, later. We ask for a small fee for the night.'

'Yes, I understand. I just – missed my flight, couldn't get into a hotel …'

'Look, we don't need to know your circumstances, other than that you have nowhere to sleep tonight. That wound on your arm suggests you're not a freeloading businessman.' He smiled briefly at his own use of irony. Jan sat on the bottom bunk, exhausted, but in pain, and reluctant to lie down and feel the swimming in his head overpower him. The man opposite him looked at him, without speaking.

Jan felt too tired to speak. He looked at the man, tried to smile, but felt that any attempt at conversation would be irrelevant.

The man looked away slowly. After a while, his gaze fixed on the makeshift wall behind Jan, the man said, with a heavy Slavic intonation: 'I know what happened.'

Jan was silent.

The man shrugged.

'You were lucky. He had to pay.'

Jan could not speak.

'He's in with the wrong crowd. For money. A lot of it, he thinks, but he doesn't know the truth. He will be used, like all of them.'

Jan felt an urgent need to follow this.

'Who is using them?'

'You don't want to know.'

'Please – I need to know.'

'I'm not saying any more - forget it.'

'So, where can I find out more?'

'What's it worth?'

'I have 250 kruna left. That's all I've got.'

'I don't believe you. What can I do with that? But I'll take it. Now.'

Jan handed over the crumpled notes.

'Smichov. Down between the rail station, and the old casino. But you'd be an idiot to go down there. You'll get more than a little cut on your arm.'

The man fell into a sudden and noisy sleep. Jan tried to rest, fitfully, on his sound arm.
He woke next day to find that his phone, cards and the man had disappeared.

CHAPTER NINE. *'I say there is no darkness but ignorance.'*
(Feste, *Twelfth Night*)

'So, why do you think Bridgeworth is being so cagey about this?'
The two officers were taking a break and using it to return to their questions about the two murders.
'Oh, old issues I think, with Matthews. The word is Bridgeworth wrapped up a case that Matthews was running. To be completely honest, off the record, the other word is that Matthews was covering something up.'
'That wouldn't surprise me. He's not known for his love of sharing. Guess some would say he's just a stickler for the rule book … others would say the opposite. What about Bridgeworth?'

'Terrified of getting it wrong, on the whole. He was quick to stamp down on going beyond explaining the bodies, but if you ask me if he was too reluctant to get into the OC business. I've got a horrible feeling he suspects there's more going on than we're being told about. So – what is there that you *have* been told about?'

'Matthews definitely seems to be homing in on the drugs side. Probably better chance of getting some inside intel. What appears to be an abandoned lockup has been found in South London which was owned by Beckswith. Forensics have found evidence of items being stored there recently, but only in terms of the packaging used. Nothing to identify contents. No fingerprint evidence. But there is some CCTV footage from the main road at the end of the lockup block. An unmarked white box van, stolen number plates, three male occupants. Later clocked at a service area on the M6, nothing after that. Owner of a stolen vehicle – not a van – with the number plates reported the apparent theft three weeks prior. Nothing there. Hardly a breakthrough, but there you go.'

'We need to find just one link, don't we? Or do you think we're completely off the track here? Are we wasting our time?'

'I don't know, to be honest. How are you getting on with suspects for the Birch murder?'

'We've been through the database, got a few regulars who are not currently banged up. The most likely is a crowd in East London, run a protection scam, known to be random thugs. Plenty of previous in relation to ABH. They are the best fit at the moment, but the alibis are tricky to break. There's just not enough evidence to go further with them. It makes it harder that Birch looks so clean.'

'OK. Look mate, I think that Birch is the toughest in terms of not getting a result for the family, but if it comes to it maybe it'll have to stay as an open case until something comes up, if it does. The mystery man may not be worth pursuing.'

'You're right. You've got enough to deal with, anyway. Good luck with that, rather you than me.'
…….
Jan had returned to Prague, his wound treated and funds replenished. He had to use this as the starting point, the last place he had seen Johanna. He headed for the area of the town named by the man on the boat.
'I'm just looking for my sister.'
Jan was talking to a man on the street, in the Smichov region of the city. The man had challenged him, warned him of consequences if he started making trouble.
'And what makes you think anyone would know anything about your sister?'
'I'm just making enquiries. She left a few days ago.'
'You shouldn't get involved in anything round here. If I were you I'd get back to where you came from.'
'But if I did get involved …?'
'Get out of here. I won't warn you again.'
'But do you know anyone who might have some information?'
'I might, but I wouldn't go near them if I wanted to keep my brain inside my head. Clear off.'
Jan turned and walked away, gesturing an apology to the man. He waited behind the corner of the street, as the man disappeared from view. He had to at least try.
A grubby café at the other end of the street was empty, but open. Jan went in and asked for a coffee. The woman behind the counter glared at him, gave him a coffee wordlessly and took a few coins. Jan was determined, in spite of the silent contempt.
'I'm looking for my sister. I've been told I might get some information around here.'
The woman laughed without humour.
'Good luck with that. You won't get any help round here. This is a dangerous place, without the right backup.'

'Look, I don't care about all this stuff about danger, threats, thugs. I just want to find my sister. If I don't find the people here who can help, then I'm going to have to go to the police.'

The woman froze.

'You really are stupid, aren't you? Look, if you want to stay alive, don't ask any further. If you don't, tell the police. Or go to number 48.'

'What?'

'Number 48. Turn right out of here, go down the third road on your left, you'll see the number. But I didn't tell you that.'

Number 48 was not what he expected. Why would there be a dry cleaners in an area like this? It appeared to be in business, with racks of clothes covered in polythene waiting to be collected.

'I think we can help you, sir.'

The young man behind the counter was business-like, relaxed.

'We can offer you a turnaround of three days.'

Jan stayed silent.

'Sometimes we need to order materials from overseas for repairs.'

'Can you tell me how long it would take?'

'Let me have a look at the list.'

He referred to a sheet of paper he drew from below the counter.

'We have a few shipments coming in – let's see when we could do it for you …'

The man checked his sheet and wrote down some information on a piece of paper.

'There you go. That's the earliest date we could do for you.'

Jan looked at the sheet. It gave three dates, but in the past. They were next to flight numbers.

Jan felt a surge of what felt like panic. He couldn't think clearly. He felt he needed to get away, to find space to work this out.

'Thank you. Can I use you again?'

'We're very busy for the next few weeks, sir, we have some big events coming up. But I can give you our card.'

Jan read the card.

He thanked the man and left the shop. He had to make a plan. He now had a contact, a real link. He needed to go back to Amsterdam and prepare to take action. He looked at the card – a single word, *Simecek*, and a telephone number – and knew he must first call the number as soon as possible.

....

Simecek spoke with urgency.

'You cannot go yourself. None of us can take that risk, because we will certainly be eliminated. We have people who can do this, they can go undercover, they leave no tracks. It is a skilled job.'

'If I use one of these people, manage to pay them, what will they do?'

'Payment is not necessary. The organisation is privately funded. If payment was involved, it would then become criminalised. If we can effect a rescue, then they would go to the safe points – we have female recruits in Britain who would go into the safe houses and find the women. We would require absolute identity confirmation that would be indisputable but as secret as possible. You would need a password that your sister would understand. Your name will not be enough. They then can arrange for passports to be provided, appearance to be changed, then get them to the airport. They stop there. After that, it is for the women to decide what to do. The riskier path is to go to the Embassy or the police, but this again will not only criminalise them – they have entered the country on a forged passport – but will also risk their being found and killed.'

'So, what do the rest do?'

'They start a new life. Any qualifications they may have can be adjusted to contain their name, fake references. Some may even choose to separate from all their family and friends, to prevent being detected. Don't forget, the gangs will have their original passports, if they still exist. We need to end this call. I have to go.'

'Can you arrange someone for me? How do I keep in touch with you?'

'You never phone me again. I will call you when I need more information from you, and then when the arrangements are made.'

....

Jan was relieved to be home. To be in the centre of Amsterdam felt incongruous, safe and companionable. He had tried to watch for anyone following him, since before he left Prague, but he was exhausted with the effort, and felt that in the melee of central Amsterdam, he should be safe. He had memorised the information on the sheet and burned it. Three flights out of Amsterdam, one to Paris, and two to London. To Paris on 23rd June at 21:40, then two to London on 5th July at 06:30 and on 20th July at 18:50. He last saw Johanna on 20th July, when she was waiting to be picked up to be taken to the airport. To see it in black and white was a shock. She had definitely gone to London. His first reaction was that he had to go to London, immediately - and knew that to do so without information, without contacts, would be pointless and dangerous. He knew he could do nothing until Simecek phoned. Meanwhile, he had thought carefully about the password he would give for Johanna. It was easy – '*paarse ezel*' – purple donkey. Johanna was passionate about donkeys, and until she was a teenager had kept dozens of models in her room. When Jan had commented, 'You have donkeys in every colour except purple', she challenged him to find her one. Which he did – a crudely hand-carved one, found in a market, painted purple.

…….

'We have someone. He lives in London. We will have a woman contact at the address. She will explain the plan to Johanna, using the password. She will arrange for Johanna to be smuggled out of the location. Johanna will be provided with a new name and passport, a change of style of clothes, simple things like a change of hair colour and style. She will be taken to the airport and given a flight ticket. The rest will be up to her.'

Jan had no time to thank Simecek, as the phone disconnected.

…….

'Woodley, in here please.'

'Sir?'

'Something's come up. The Birch case.'

'What is it, sir?'

'His flat was put up for sale. I won't tell you the price, it's a Monday morning and I haven't had a coffee yet. His sister was going through the flat, checking for anything that might have got missed. The carpet in the bedroom needed to be pulled up, they were changing everything to laminate before the sale. In one corner, the carpet had been previously pulled up and refitted. In a gap between the rods and the floor was this.'

'A USB stick. It's been opened?'

'It has, forensics have had a look too. I guess the sister has, as well, and thank God she has a conscience. She phoned us; we had a constable pick it up.'

'And …?'

'The numbers on that slip of paper? They might have been flight information. Look at this.'

He inserted the device into his computer.

He opened the file labelled 'HOLIDAY PLANS'.

Dutch female. Original name Johanna. To be moved to safe location from consignment address.   Arrived UK 20/7.
Code name: Kyle.
Password: paarse ezel – DO NOT USE. To be used by contact.

Consignment location: See OS provided. UCO in situ, female.
She will arrange meet point by code text day before agreed meet
date. NO POLICE CONTACT.
Transfer to safe location and deposit.
DO NOT COMMUNICATE.

'Wow. I don't know where to start. What do you mean
about flight information?'

'Just a wild guess Woodley – but look at the numbers on
that paper again – 0581 7002 703– look at them in reverse,
307 2007 1850 – does that look like a flight time to you?'

'Go on, tell me.'

There was a flight 307 from Prague to London on 20th July
at 18:50.'

Woodley paused.

'Does this mean back to OCU?'

'I'm glad to say, it does.'

CHAPTER TEN *'Come not between the dragon and his wrath.'* (Lear, *King Lear*.)

Jan could not settle.

He knew that he should not phone Simecek. But he also knew that he would be wise not to assume anything. He had told his parents that Johanna was well, was very busy in Britain, and would be in touch soon. This was unbearable, but not as much as telling them that she had been taken by criminals, and they were not to contact the police at any cost. His only hope was to find her himself. He told his boss that he must deal with family problems, would be back, and would accept the cut in pay. He had to contact Simecek and ask how he could join the group. Simecek was scornful, and irritated.

'Why do you not trust us? It is in hand. We have ways of retrieving the women. It is too dangerous for anyone to travel there and be involved.'

'But if I am a member of the group, I will have the power to be part of the rescue – and my sister will trust me.'

'This is not a child's game, with taking sides, acting out the victim and the hero.'

'I can't stay here.'

'And you can't go there.'

'Maybe not as a member of the group, then. But I will go.'
....

'Can you tell me a little about yourself? I don't mind if you can't.'

Jane was still gazing out of the window. They were now on the motorway, and she hadn't spoken during the journey, too fearful that she would not be able to control her emotions.

'I am from Amsterdam. I can't believe that I was so stupid. But there was nothing at that end to suggest anything wrong.'

'That's exactly how they con people, intelligent women like yourself, mainly. That's why we're doing everything we can to break down their system.'

'Are you managing it?'

'You're here, aren't you? Every single rescue is important, part of the goal. I don't know if we'll succeed. To have insider connections is valuable, even when it is so dangerous. But they are powerful, for all the wrong reasons. Money drives everything.'

'I am very grateful. Will they try to find me?'

'They'll probably try, which is why you'll be given another name, a new passport and an airline ticket. We can't tell you what to do, but we strongly advise you to take great care once you have these. It will be your responsibility then. I am taking you to a safe location, where you can stay for 48 hours while we arrange the documents. Then I will pick you up and take you to have a few changes to your appearance, very basic, so you're not immediately recognisable. Then we'll go to the airport for your flight. It will not be in London, to minimise the risk. Oh, I have something of yours. Unfortunately, I have forgotten to bring it. The call came suddenly, I'm sorry, I forgot. They had left a message with the details of your incoming flight, and a code word to confirm their identity, and a possession of yours.'

'My rosary. They took that from me.'

'That was the undercover police officer. She is working with us and took that from you under pretence of locking it away. She had to send something that she knew belonged to you, and you would recognise. She managed to get that sent out to us. I hid it in the flat, and in my rush forgot to get it. I'm really sorry. It hasn't worked quite according to plan, but I think I can say you have recognised it – it was so I would know you were the right person, and you would know I was who I say I am.'

'My grandmother gave that to me, just before she died. It's OK, it is not that important, as you have saved my life. My grandmother would have forgiven you!'

'I can't risk bringing it to the house, as there is a small risk it will be used to identify you. I will find a way of getting it to you.'

'And these people – who you work for. Who are they?'

'A group committed to ending the trade in trafficking. Some of them have relatives who have died as a result of it. And quite a few of them put themselves at significant risk, infiltrating the gangs and getting information. And of course, the police are interested in what we do, whether we can pass on anything. This particular gang, the police have been after for some time. We've been able to pass on information about locations – in return, they have provided us with information about individual cases, especially when there is a fault in the plans – you escaping, for example. The police officer contacted us straight away, with information about where we could find you.'

'Why didn't she just use her police colleagues?'

'Because it was far too risky. If the police picked you up, her cover would be completely blown. The gang would have known and she would have been disposed of straight away. We had to get you out as discreetly as possible.'

'I am very grateful for all these people. Why do they risk themselves?'

'I don't know, to be honest. Maybe it's altruism.'

'And is that the case for you?'

He paused.

'Someone's got to do something.'

…….

Jan had spent too long weighing up the pros and cons of risking himself, or of risking his sister, or of achieving the best outcome, with them both returning home, safely. He would use his passport to enter the country, and then destroy it. If all went well, then he would just go through the process of reporting a lost passport. In the event of things going wrong, he had arranged for communication to be sent to his parents, confirming how he may be identified, that they can then pass to the police. He had organised this in such a way that he would be able to intercept the message before he returned to Amsterdam. He would take one precious item with him, one thing that would confirm to Jo, if no-one else, that he came to find her, just in case he is able to make contact with the group. He would go to London, and he would look for any links with the group. After his experience in Prague, maybe he should start with shelters – he was not likely to be welcomed by any women's groups. And he could call Simecek. Surely he would relent, and let him have some information.

He had arranged to stay in a small guest house, where he would use his passport to register before 'losing' it.

He had visited London before, and had a grasp of its cosmopolitan, idiosyncratic and individualistic nature. He knew that turning a corner would often produce an anomaly or a novelty, and that this was the way to discover the food bank next to the library, or the university department hidden in a high and narrow street of former warehouses. One of the most historically diverse cities in the western world, London was a rich source of contact with every sphere of society. Surely, he would be able to seek out the displaced.

The Westfield Social Club was the venue, on Wednesday nights, of the support for the homeless group run by the Salvation Army. The temporary sign at the door said: WESTFIELD COMMUNITY SUPPORT. ALL ARE WELCOME. PLEASE KNOCK.

It was 8.00 in the evening, and the large room was steamy and warm. The users – or guests, as the hosts referred to them – were mainly young, some with battered guitars or old rucksacks, covered with faded badges. A further sign above the long table read:

DRUGS AND ALCOHOL ARE NOT PERMITTED ON SITE. ANYONE FOUND IN POSSESSION OF SAME WILL BE POLITELY ASKED TO LEAVE. SMOKING IS NOT ALLOWED ON THE PREMISES.

The young people were quietly seated, some in groups on the floor, some using the cheap folding plastic chairs which lined the room. Most had plates of food on their laps, while some leaned back and dozed against the nearest upright surface. Many were gazing into the empty middle distance. The atmosphere was of quiet despair.

In contrast, the confident and motherly woman who approached Jan projected what could only be described as a light in the darkness. She actually seemed to glow. She gestured Jan into the room and asked if he would like some food and tea.

'That's very kind of you, but I am fine. I just wanted to have a look, if that's not rude.'

'Of course not. Sometimes people pop in out of curiosity and go out with something they didn't realise they needed.'

She paused.

'Or sometimes they end up becoming volunteers, or go out muttering that it's disgusting that people are getting something for nothing.'

She laughed with warm vigour.

'I actually heard someone say *A spell in the Army would do them the world of good*.'

She smiled.

'We live in a very insular world, I think.'

Jan instantly liked this woman and felt he should perhaps change his mind about looking for information.

'So, what is it you want to know?'

Jan felt the woman again had second guessed him, and she didn't mind.

'I'm sorry if I come across as being intrusive. I'm just looking for my sister, who I believe his been kidnapped.'

The woman's face became grave, with genuine sympathy.

'Please, why don't you come and sit over here, out of the way of the clutter? I promise I won't try to convert you.' She smiled.

Her unselfconscious honesty was gentle and engaging.

'Tell me about your sister.'

'She is from Amsterdam. I believe she has been brought to Britain, London in particular, under false pretences, on the promise of work. I don't know where she is.'

Jan was alarmed to feel emotion gripping his chest.

The woman sat silently.

'I've got to find her. I will take any risk.'

'These people are very dangerous. I have known many people disappear. I feel you could really take a different path and just give it to the police.'

She would not use the words ought, should, must. She knew that to judge was counterproductive.

'It's impossible. She might even already be dead. Any police involvement will make things worse.'

'Please, you cannot make them better. Anything you do now to try and get involved, will take you down a path that will get more and more complicated and dangerous. Maybe you could return to Amsterdam and see if the authorities can help from there? Sometimes involving your Embassy will give you protection from the risks.' She paused again.

'But I cannot tell you what to do. I can pray for you. It can make me feel better knowing I've done it, and you feel better knowing someone cares. Maybe that's what prayer is.' She laughed warmly.

Jan noted she did not say that she would pray for him. He appreciated that.

'But I want you to take care. There are too many statistics out there.'

The woman watched Jan walk back up the street, and her heart ached.

…..

At the end of the street, a small group of restless men huddled in conversation. It would seem they had been watching Jan leave the centre, and had made efforts to appear that they hadn't, pretending to notice him just as he was walking up the street. On his approach, a man with greasy, unkempt hair and cold, sallow skin looked up, with a gap-toothed, soulless grin, and dull, empty, yellowed eyes.

'Are you looking for something good, man?'

'No, I am not. I'm not interested. Excuse me.'

'Sure, no worries, man. You just looked like someone who could do with a good fix, unless you're looking for something else?'

The man's grin became even more stiff and skeletal, as he leaned towards Jan conspiratorially.

Jan paused, and looked at the man.

'I don't want anything, get out of the way.'

'Hey, man! It's cool. No hassle. You know where to come then, if you do. Just don't leave it too long.'

'What do you mean?'

The other men, not seeing an easy sale, had wandered off, sharing roll-ups in the entrance of a derelict arcade.

'I mean, you won't find anything by going the legal route, if you know what I mean. You gotta get to the big guys.'

'What big guys?'

The main put on a wheedling, sarcastic tone.

'Oh, what big guys? Oh, *those* big guys - the ones who can get anything you want. At a price.'

'Do you have a name?'

His experience in Prague nagged him.

'Ha! Think I'm some kind of loser? You get to the big guys, and you're dead. That's how you pay the price, little boy.'

Jan was tiring of the rambling, inconsequential, affected arrogance of the man, and started to move away.

The man grabbed him by the arm, with startling physical strength.

'Look, you wanna find someone, you gotta turn around and go back to wherever you came from. The only way they'll let you find what you're looking for is by destroying you first. But hey, you wanna do that, you do that. Loser.'

The other men had turned and were approaching, focused now and no longer dissimulating.

Jan knew that to turn and run would be the ultimate folly. 'I've no idea what you're talking about. Now move, before I call the police.'

'What, on the phone I could nick off you before you'd got it in your hands? Loser!!'

The man's face showed first scorn, then humour, and finally resignation. Mental energy was spent. Suddenly, he seemed to have no mood for playing games, as if the effort of intimidation had drained him of life. He and his acquaintances wandered off, undirected and distant.

Jan returned to his lodgings, unsure how he could locate anyone who would be able to help and realising that it might have been naïve to assume that it would be easy. It also occurred to him, that if he made his plans known, and his identity, then he would be putting himself in more danger, that may risk Johanna's safety.

The guesthouse was run by a humourless woman, who had long since realised that guests were not to be trusted, or had no sense of decency, or both. She knocked on his door, and without ceremony handed him a sealed note which had been delivered that day.

'We don't normally act as a postal address, Mr de Hoek. In this case, however, as it was hand delivered, I'm happy to pass this on, just this once.'

'Thank you very much, Mrs Godwin. Did you notice who delivered it?'

'It was given to the cleaner. I'm afraid I don't know any more than that.'

'I appreciate it, Mrs Godwin. I will be leaving in a few days, by the way.'

He took the note, closed the door, and sat on the narrow bed in the cramped, overcrowded room.

'Do not keep looking. You need to speak to me only. Our Prague contacts told us to look for you. This evening at 8.00, leave the guest house, turn left and go to the end of the street. Turn left again, and you will see a McDonald's 50 metres down the road. Go in there, order your food and take it to the table in the corner of the window. I will be waiting for you. Destroy this note.'

....

Jan knew that he had to be absolutely sure that he was approaching the right person. He waited until he had caught the eye of the man seated at the table.

The man looked away almost instantly, but laid his hand out flat upon the table, palm downwards, and kept it there while continuing to look fixedly out of the window.

'Just sit down, and don't speak.' The man didn't move his head away from the street scene outside.

Jan placed his tray on the table and tried to relax his grip as he took a sip of his coffee.

'We can locate your sister. We have to remove her from the current location, however, and this will be very difficult. I can do this, but I will probably be killed if I do so. For the moment, we have to wait until we can formulate a plan. But she is alive.'

'Is she being held?'

'Of course. If she tries to escape, she will be killed also. We just need to work on contacts who have access.'

'How do you know about her ... me?'

'The passports were taken from them. A contact overheard your enquiry at the centre. It was easy to find out your name – I followed you to your lodgings, and when you were out I asked if a Mr Brown – any name – was staying. The woman said no, I made some story that he probably hadn't arrived yet and I asked her to check if any mail had arrived in that name. While she was gone, I looked in the registration book. Yours was the only name written during the last three days. It was then easy to link this with your sister's, of course.'

'So you are – what, a mole? An agent?'

'It is critical that you don't reveal anything of this meeting – anything, at all. I am of no importance. But if I'm discovered, then I will be killed, probably tortured first.'

'So, why …?'

'Because I am working with an organisation that saves these women. But I also work with the gang. So I cannot risk being found.'

'So, what can I do?'

'I must be able to trace your sister precisely. Is there anything you can tell me that will identify her?'

'She … She is called Johanna de Hoek.'

'We cannot risk using any real names. Is there anything, something of hers that you have, something small?'

Jan froze.

'I have it here. With me.'

'What is it?'

'It's a small toy – I wanted to bring it, so she would know …'

'And she would recognise it?'

'Categorically.'

Jan brought the small donkey out of his pocket.

'Let me have it. I will use it to recognise her.'

Jan paused.

'How do I know …?'

'By realising you have no choice.'

The man stood up to leave, affecting a smile for the first time, and offering a brief nod to Jan.

CHAPTER ELEVEN   *'Why then tonight let us assay our plot.'*   (Helena, *All's Well That Ends Well*)

'I think you'll agree, this is more than a straightforward murder enquiry now.'
Bridgenorth looked down at Matthews, seated at his desk. 'I agree. Maybe it's a matter for us to take over, John. We can't risk anything getting in the way of the contacts we have in the OCG.'

'Which are …?'

'Really? You know I can't reveal that sort of information. We've already lost one officer. We've got one more undercover inside the group. A male. The group are using him to negotiate transport, pickups from the docks. Fairly minor stuff, a cover mainly. Gets the documents authenticated. And he's getting information about the big stuff. But that's as far as I'll go.'

'So how does this link to our two bodies?'

'What it does, is relieve you of the responsibility.'

'Not good enough, Rob. My duty has been to finish these two jobs. My DCI will not be happy if I say it's an OCU job and sorry, but we can't take it any further.'

'It is what it is. Look, if I get anything that shows these two deaths aren't linked, then sure, I'll send them back to you.'

'Are you going to tell me anything about where you're at with it right now?'

'We're getting close. That's all I can risk saying at the moment.'

…….

'So what's going on, sir?'

'OCU think they're taking it over. Without more information, I'm not happy.'

'So, what next?'

'Look, can you just do a bit more of a push on what's known about the group? Are they *Podzim*? Is there any way we can get information about the location of the consignment property? What was Birch doing on the A120 when he would presumably normally use the motorway to get from Cambridge to London? Was he coming from Cambridge, or going to Cambridge, or going to or from somewhere else? Was he on the way to or from the airport? Was he on the way to or from the coast? CCTV footage at petrol stations, roadside eateries? I know it's clutching at straws, but there must be something we've missed. He can't be completely squeaky clean. This was a targeted assault, I'm certain. If we can at least get a reason for it, we might be on the way to getting information about the perpetrators. I don't think we can go any further with the chap on the beach. But I think I might take another trip down there. Come with me, Woodley, we might need to do some probing down there.'
....
Matthews and the UCO had chosen a country pub, 40 miles away from the city and many more from the east coast to talk over the case.
'They talk about the triangle, sir. Since the fire, they've had a shakeup of personnel. After Gregor's death, they've brought in a gang of three from the hub in Amsterdam. Two men are in charge of the transit from further east, have set up a new processing system. Got rid of the arrival setup. The women are just taken straight to the houses. They're trying to cut out all possibilities for any contamination, any information leak. The other man is the money man. He doesn't actually do much other than hold on to the cash. But he could certainly hold his ground if needed.'
'Names?'

'First names only – and probably false. Radek and Anton,
Josef is the money man. So the central group now are
those three, Jakub Rusu and Vulpe. They are still moving
all the time. We've been in and out of London, up to
Durham, Manchester, down to Salisbury.'
'Now?'
'London. Big operation coming up.'
'Right. I want you at the centre. Watch yourself as usual,
but if you can get a stable location we can set up an
operation of our own. We're going to need to act instantly
on this. I want them all in one place and ideally isolated.'
'it's imminent, sir. This triangle business is important. It
seems to be maintaining the system. I can't get into the
group, I don't get any prior information, I just have to
move things when they tell me. I don't know what the
triangle is, a place, people, I've no idea.'
'Is there anything you can do to get that information? Is
there a price worth paying?'
'The problem is it's likely it's only known by the core
group, sir. Maybe just Rusu and Vulpe. Any attempt to
get that information will be highly suspicious. Vulpe
particularly is hot on controlling how much people know.'
'OK. Let's get back to business.'
…….
'I don't like them being brought in.'
Jakub Rusu was walking without purpose between the
pillars of the derelict parking lot.
Vulpe was seated on a metal box, crumbling a roll-up
between his fingers.
'We have no choice. We need to move things faster, so we
need more people. They have been checked.'
'What good is checking? Look at what happened to the
house. What good was checking then, if the police can get
in and snoop around – who knows what she got across to
the bosses. They are starting to get close to intercepting
our key handover points. Which suggests she wasn't the
only one.'

'So we kill everyone, yes? You too?'

Vulpe stood slowly and confronted the other man.

'Ha! So you want to call it a day, you haven't got the courage to dig them out, is that so? You want to end up in a pit, with no one to recognise you and put you in a grave?'

Vulpe grabbed the man suddenly and held him in an arm lock against the concrete wall.

'Without me, you'd have been in a pit, long before your brother.'

The other man reddened, roared in fury, and went to wrench Vulpe away, but suddenly dropped, and fell to the floor.

Vulpe knew it was now over. These three men were coming, and with the brothers out of the way, and the hub of the group crumbled away like dust, and with the blame inevitably placed on him, he could no longer stay. He was marked.

. . . .

'I'm on duty, but I wouldn't say no to just one lager top. Thank you. You too, Woodley?'

Bridgeworth and Woodley were standing at the bar of The Ship.

'I can't really tell you any more than you know, Inspector. He was just someone who seemed interested in the incident. He really wasn't the only one. We get the locals, imagining all sorts of criminal activity on the island, the visitors, who want a bit of salubrious gossip, and the press, who want to make more of it than it is.'

'More than it is?'

'An unknown man, no history, washed up on the beach? Have you been down to slot machine city, Inspector?'

'Well, it's certainly a possibility, he could be a vagrant, or an addict. But people don't usually end up in the sea, without a reason. Usually someone has seen something.'

'Maybe you're right. My guess he hasn't got any family or friends who'd care, though.'

'So why did you feel it was of note, sir?'

'Sorry?'

'The man who was enquiring. You mentioned it to one of your regulars. They seemed to think you were suspicious about him.'

'A community like this loves a bit of danger, Inspector. Can you imagine living on this island? Not exactly LA, is it?'

'So, your job involves a little bit of stirring then, is that right?'

'Call it entertainment, Inspector. Better than what you can get on the TV these days.'

'So, are you saying you invented this suspicious stranger?'

'Not exactly. Let's say I just added a bit of colour.'

'I see. Well, thank you for your time, Mr Hardwicke. If you do see or hear anything – actually significant – which might throw some light on this unfortunate incident, I'm sure you'll let us know?'

'Will do, Inspector.'

....

'Of course, Inspector, come in. Gail has gone back to Birmingham for now, but I'm happy to answer any further questions. Have you got any more information about the poor man?'

'I'm afraid not, Mrs Pendleton. We're just checking up on whether anything has occurred to anyone, anything they had forgotten and has just come back …? It's surprising how things can come back, after a few weeks have elapsed.'

'I really don't think so. Not really. But … after calling the other day, I didn't want to waste any more of your time …'

She hesitated.

'Please don't worry, Judith. If it's irrelevant, I assure you it's normal – our job is to sort the wheat from the chaff, as it were. We're used to it.'

'I've been thinking about the discovery of the body. It was 2nd September. Then I've been thinking about this man at the pub, and how things have been here since then. But I haven't been thinking about *before* that day.'

'What do you mean, Judith?'

'Well, up to now, it's as if everything *started* with the body …'

'But it didn't …?'

"I've been thinking about the days before …'

'So there was something before you both found the body? That you think might be related?'

'Or may not, Inspector. That's the point – it could have been completely normal …'

'Judith, we've already had something normal which was deliberately made out to be suspicious – I'd be very happy if something which seemed ordinary was actually significant …'

'I just saw a lorry on the island. There, that's it. Sounds stupid, doesn't it?'

'It depends. There must have been something that you felt was unusual – did it have any markings, did you see anyone, was it driving erratically …?'

'It wasn't the lorry itself, exactly. It was what it was doing.'

He waited.

'It was reversing. Down on the shoreline. Why would it be doing that?'

'When was this?'

'I think my mind must be making something more of it than there really is. It just seemed odd. It was before the body was found – I can't remember when, but I know I was thinking about Gail visiting. I've been doing a bit of tutoring, young people on the island, preparing for entrance exams. I remember thinking that it would be good when Gail got down, and the pre-uni rush was over, and it would be quiet.'

'Can you be a little more precise about the date?'

'I can. As I said, it was before Gail was due … thinking about it, it could only have been two days before. I know I was off the island the day before that. I'd been on the mainland, doing some shopping, for Christmas and for Gail's stay, I didn't go off the island again after I got home.'

'What did you think about the lorry at the time?'

'Well, nothing, really – I just thought it was a strange thing to do. People occasionally launch small boats from cars, or 4x4s. But I didn't see anything like that. And I thought it was odd that …'

Bridgeworth was silent, and Judith felt she couldn't retract.

'Geoff was there.'

'Geoff …?'

'Geoff Hardwicke. The barman. At The Ship.'

'What was he doing?"

'I can only guess was directing them. He was standing near the breakers, waving them back. Then nothing happened.'

'I'm sorry?'

'Well, obviously, something must have happened, but I felt a bit conspicuous – for some reason, I felt it wouldn't be good if they saw me. I didn't see the men in the lorry. The windows were dark, tinted. I just saw Geoff get in the back of the lorry, and I went home. It is just over the last few days, I've worried about it. Obviously, to be frank with you, I'm worried they had the body in the lorry. But it could have been anything. And I realised I could have been – well, reading too much into it – again. They could have been tidying up the beach, for all I know. That's common at the end of the summer. And Geoff sometimes helps with that. That's why it never really occurred to me that it could be anything serious.'

'But you felt anxious? Didn't want to be seen?'

'I can't really say why. If I try and analyse it, maybe it's because it didn't look like the usual type of refuse collection lorry that they use on the island, or because it was dusk and it seemed an odd time of day – I really don't know. I'm not a melodramatic person, I believe in Occam's razor.'

'I beg your pardon …?'

'The simplest solution is more likely to be the correct one.'

'Quite. I'm sure that's the case here, but please rest assured we don't dismiss anything. We really do appreciate any information – it's our job to sort it all out. Thank you for your time. We'll leave you in peace.'

Judith watched the two men walk away up the road, to the pub car park where they had left the car. She didn't feel any better.

…….

Bridgeworth sat in the bar, not quite ready to get home. He wanted to think, but neither work nor home were the right place to do it. A quiet and nondescript pub, on a Wednesday evening, seemed about right. He took his pint to a chair at a small table and went over the points he had to work with. He couldn't get away from this business of the triangle. Why was it bothering him so much? What was niggling? Is it the bit that holds everything together? Is it even people – is it to do with corrupt organisations, Big Pharma maybe? He hadn't had that much contact with OCGs, only the fruits of their activities. So Vulpe – Andrei – was possibly the island body, was in with both sides, maybe an undercover for the rescue group, maybe was using a codename or just an alias. Or maybe he'd just passed on information. He couldn't be Matthews' UCO, as apparently he was still on the job. One of the gang had died in the fire. Another UCO was present and died in the fire. Amsterdam weren't keen to get involved. Birch was possibly involved in the trafficking, note on USB mentioned a Dutch woman, possible flight time from Prague, password, a man's name, the undercover officer. So – was Vulpe a contact? Was Birch a courier, or a rescuer? And then there was Hardwicke - what's he up to? Is that just a random incident, getting in the way? And what was the one thing which sat on the periphery, nagging at him, beyond all these questions?

He realised he hadn't got any further. He was an assiduous and reliable senior officer, but he also liked his own space. Time to go home.

....

He had forgotten to set the heating. Bridgeworth shrugged in resignation and pushed the boost. The bottle of wine and the gradually warming flat didn't manage to distract him from his uneasy thoughts. He had to somehow separate out all the individual facts and try and rebuild the picture from the ground up. He had to put aside the triangle, first of all. It was insubstantial and unevidenced. The next thing was to let go of the assumptions - the implied links, the tenuous facts about OCGs. It felt that the only concrete evidence he had were the testimonies of the women who had found the first body, and confirmation that the second body died as a result of an assault.

Just letting himself put aside the complexities and hearsay freed him to relax. He didn't always enjoy this moment - he liked to have his brain working, not distracted by his own thoughts, and the solitude of the flat. But it usually passed, and that was the point when he realised he needed to sleep. And in that moment, it happened. He knew.

CHAPTER TWELVE   *'It's not enough to speak, but to speak true.'* (Lysander, *A Midsummer Night's Dream*)

'Thank you for agreeing to give us some more of your time, Mr Hardwicke.'

'Geoff, please. We have to do what we can to help. The incident has caused a lot of gossip on the island. I don't know how I can add anything, though.'

The Ship was quiet on a midweek early evening, and the barman wiped his hands and leant on the bar.

'Well, some information has come to light which does connect with you. I'd like to just know a little more about it.'

'Information?'

'Let's forget about the so-called suspicious stranger for now, Mr Hardwicke. We've been made aware of other activities on the island which you might possibly know about.'

'I'm sure I've told you everything I can, Inspector. As I said, I'm sorry if I fed a bit of gossip on the island – there really hasn't been anything going on that I've been aware of.'

'Well, according to some information that has come to light, it appears you have been busy on the island, what with all the work involved in running the pub … keeping the customers happy …'

'Look, I'm very sorry for wasting your time. I know I shouldn't get involved with the petty interests of the islanders. It just livens things up a bit. I'll hold back in future.'

'That's not really my concern, Mr Hardwicke, if we don't have anything to worry about in respect of this stranger. I'm just a bit more interested in the lorry.'

'I'm sorry? What lorry? The delivery lorries? As far as I'm aware, they're all legit and above board, although it's not my job to check all that - I leave it to the brewery …''

'Oh, I'm sure they're all fine, sir. It's a specific lorry I'm interested in.'

'Look, you've lost me. I don't know anything about a lorry.'

'It may have been a truck, or a box van, or a flatbed, I don't know – but I do know you were seen in connection with one. On the evening of 31st August this year, if you can cast your mind back. Two nights before the body was found.'

Hardwicke paused, before answering, his voice lower. He moved the empty glasses under the counter. He glanced up again, a tolerant smile covering his discomfort.

'I really have no idea what you mean.'

'You know your regulars and locals well? A busy and successful pub in a small village usually does very well for its regular visitors – it's a bit like a weekly routine for many, isn't it? Drop into the local of a Friday or Saturday night?'

'Of course.'

'How long have you been the landlord of The Ship?'

'Must be nearly 15 years now.'

"You like the job?'

'Of course. Who wouldn't? Nice environment, good business … but what is this to do with anything?'

'Presumably it goes both ways – your regulars get to know you well?'

'Look, I really don't know what's going on. I've explained the story behind the stranger, and I'm very sorry if it's caused problems, wasted your time. I just don't understand what you mean about a lorry – I get deliveries several times a week, it's always been OK …'

'Let's forget the deliveries. I'm more interested in - shall we say - disposals? Can you remember that night, two nights before the body was found on the beach?'

'What? No, not specifically. Look, I'm really busy, I've told you, I don't know anything about some random lorry … Are you accusing me of something? My business is legitimate …'

'Mr Hardwicke, you're not under caution and we're not making any accusations, at the moment. You're free to answer or refuse to answer any questions you wish. This is just a chat. So, two nights before the discovery? A Friday, if that helps.'

'I would have been cashing up, and checking the barrels. But I can't remember that specific Friday. I only heard about the body a few days later, I guess.'

'So you don't remember being involved in helping with a vehicle that evening?'

'No, this is stupid, of course I don't, why would I? Helping with a vehicle? Look, I need to get ready for this evening's opening. Have we finished?'

'Of course, sir. But as this is an enquiry into a crime, I can't guarantee we won't need to speak to you again. Have a good evening, sir.'

Bridgeworth glanced at Woodley as they sat in the car. 'Well?'

'Suggests Mrs Pendleton was not mistaken. If it wasn't Hardwicke, he possibly wouldn't have been rattled.'

'Some people go into guilty mode even if they're not guilty, when they get a policeman in front of them. I don't like him, but nor can I prejudge anything, if he won't talk. He may have been helping out with a bit of low level smuggling, if it was him. Or he may have been helping to dump a body. Well … another one to add into the mix. Is there any chance of getting another witness or two to the lorry situation? If we can get just one more ID, or some evidence, we might have grounds for pulling him in. Let me see if I can get a Code C. Check with the local authority, what are their rules for accessing the beach by motor vehicle. It may be a long shot, but there may be something there. Did anyone report any unusual activity? Can you get down here again Woodley, ask around a bit?'

…….

'In fact, local byelaws prohibit access by vehicles larger than a class B vehicle with a small trailer. People use this means for launching small craft, with a low power outboard motor at the most, and they have to apply for a one-off permit. We certainly don't allow lorries, large vans, vehicles of that type. The ecosystem is very fragile. I can have a look and see if anything has been reported in?'

'That would be really helpful. Thank you.'

The woman searched her computer and made a few notes. 'Nothing specific has been reported for the period you mentioned … I'll just look at the permit applications, see if anything comes up there … it was a quiet summer actually, the weather wasn't very reliable, a lot of … oh, here we are. We had two permit requests in August. One was granted for the 15th – an island resident, requested a permit to launch a small sailing craft. The other, requested on the 25th, was rejected – a request to access via the causeway, which is usually only permitted for business vehicles. And the vehicle would have exceeded our limits anyway.'

'Do you happen to have any names?'

'We normally keep customer information confidential.'

'I understand. But we are looking into a serious crime, and if we can't have access now then I can go through the process of applying for a warrant to obtain the information.'

'Of course. The first was for a Ms Maeve Keighley. The permit was granted and as far as I'm aware there were no problems. The second was in the name of G. Hardwicke.'

'Do you recall what the details of the vehicle were? Why it was outside the limits?'

'I'm afraid not. I didn't take the booking, and the decision would have been made via a different system.'

'I see. Could you print off a copy of the details for me, please? I think that gives me some information. Thank you very much, er … Jackie. You've been very helpful.'

....

'I can only assume the permit application was a way of making the activity look legit, Woodley. If it had been granted, and anyone reported it, it would have been cleared by the council. But this may well be enough, especially as the permit wasn't granted. I think, based on what Jackie said, we can assume it was rejected on the basis that it wasn't a class B, and by inference was a large vehicle. We've eliminated Ms Keighley, so I think we can have him in under caution. It is too close in time to the event of the body being found. The date is puzzling me. Suggests the gang were looking ahead – this wasn't an impulse action. Presumably they were planning the murder, if that's what it was. Arrange for him to be brought in, under arrest if he refuses, the usual recommendations.'

....

'Present are Geoffrey Hardwicke, DI Bridgeworth, DS Woodley, and legal counsel Mr Thomas Uckley.

'You remain under caution, Mr Hardwicke. You've been brought in today to answer some questions surrounding events which took place on or around 31st August this year. We appreciate you have agreed to come in voluntarily and are currently not under arrest. However, if the procedure of the interview leads us to believe that you are guilty of a criminal offence, then we will take the appropriate action. Do you understand?'

'Yes, but …'

'Please just answer the questions for the moment, Mr Hardwicke. You will have plenty of opportunity to raise any issues. Based on our earlier interview with you, you stated that you were not aware of unusual activity involving a lorry or other large vehicle on the island on or around 31st August this year. Do you still state this to be true?'

'No comment.'

'DS Woodley then obtained evidence from the offices of Quayside Valley County Council that you requested a permit to access the beach by vehicle at or around the end of August 2021. Could you explain this, please?'
'No comment.'
'We have the documentary evidence to prove that this permit was requested in your name, Mr Hardwicke. Can you explain that?'
Geoff Hardwicke glanced at his solicitor.
'No comment.'
'Do you realise, Mr Hardwicke, that we have a witness who saw you, and confirmed your identity, to the effect that you were assisting in the movement of a large vehicle, which was reversing towards the water's edge, on the evening of 31st August? This sounds like a bit of a coincidence, wouldn't you say, if it wasn't you who requested the permit, but someone using your name?'
'I … it was … I didn't know anything about it …'
'About what, sir?'
'I was … told it was a quick job, getting rid of some waste. I thought it was … well, I don't know what I thought it was.'
He glanced again at his solicitor and ignored his warning gesture.
'So, you were there, but what were you doing?'
'I arranged the vehicle. I help out – get equipment on the side, that sort of thing.'
'What did you help out with on that evening?'
Uckley leaned forward.
'I must advise my client at this point, Inspector.'
'No, I'm OK with this.' Hardwicke raised a hand.
'If you're sure, Mr Hardwicke, but I must advise …'
'I don't need the advice.'
'Go on, Mr Hardwicke. You were saying you were helping out - what with?'

'I thought it was pretty innocent, just a bit off the record, if you like. Some people wanted a bit of a dump to take place. I thought it was just rubbish, or something. Too expensive to get done legitimately.'

'Who were these people?'

'I don't really know. They didn't give names.'

'Just offered you money? Didn't you have any suspicions?'

'No. It's … not that uncommon.'

'So why did they need you? Didn't they have enough people?'

'Protection. Keeping the locals away. Keeping it local, looking normal. Keeping it … hidden.'

'Looks like you didn't do a great job of keeping it that hidden. What else did you do?'

'Nothing. I didn't know what … as I said, it could have been rubbish …'

'And what was it actually?'

'I … don't know …'

'So what could it have been?'

'I don't know … I think it was a body.'

'Think it was?'

'It was. A man.'

'Mr Hardwicke, I need a lot more information to find out what was going on, and I assure you this will be continuing for some time ahead, but for now, Geoffrey Hardwicke, I am arresting you for being an accessory to illegal disposal of a body, although I expect we will be dealing with a lot more in future interviews. Owing to the serious nature of the crime, you will be detained for a period of 24 hours with the possibility of extension, for the purpose of assisting in the continuation of our enquiries, at the conclusion of which you may be charged and committed for trial.'

Uckley closed his folder, and looked troubled.

…….

'I think we've got something, sir.'

DS Harris knocked quickly, then pushed open the door of Matthews' office without ceremony.

'Caroline. We've found intel.'

'Go for it.'

'On the personal drive of her computer. A list of names.'

'And?'

'Two columns, sir. One, we know to be gang members, at least – Gregor, Jakub, Andrei, Radek, Anton, Josef. Is Andrei, Andrei Vulpe? Also The other column, unknown – Kyle, Andrei, Hana. Then, X and Y, and a question mark next to each.'

'Anything else?'

'A diagram of sorts. At the top, Cisar and Keizer, linked by a double line. Then a line and arrow from each of those to Andrei. Then a line from Andrei to Kyle. That's it. No other names on the diagram.'

Matthews paused.

'So it looks like we have a double agent maybe; Andrei, if it's the same person – but DC Kemble wouldn't have failed to indicate a difference. The name Kyle was on the note left on Birch's USB stick. Let's get CID in on it.'

…..

Bridgworth and Woodley were pulling together the information.

'Kyle was given as a codename. We could assume this is a codename to be used by Birch. If that's true, then Birch was outside the OCG. So if Andrei was acting on both sides, presumably the right hand column is AAS activists? So who is Hana? And who are Cisar and Keizer?'

'If I may add something, sir – I've been a bit into these foreign names, looking for any meanings that might help – '

'Knew I could trust you, Woodley …'

'Cisar and Keizer both mean 'emperor', or 'leader', in Czech and Dutch.'

'So Cisar is a Czech link, and Keizer Dutch?'

'That's right, sir.'

'And according to that diagram, they seem to be overseeing the operation in some way? Or a bit of it?'

'I guess we can assume they are involved in some way in the running of the operation. But somehow they are also linked. How? They must have some power to be able to contain what is a dangerous situation.'

'But isn't that the point, Woodley? Just think of it? If you have a rival who is as powerful as you – not just in terms of arms, or manpower – wouldn't you want to work with them, instead of against them? But who are X and Y? The landlord? Unknown collaborators?'

'And so where does the pub landlord come in?'

'Hired help, maybe. They have a small army of them, surely. Happy to do the dirty work for a large fee. Talking of which, I'll think we'll do a bit of background on him. I don't really see him as a crime lord, to be honest. Bit too sly, too lazy, for that. It's a real shame Caroline wasn't able to get more. There's always the other UCO, but Matthews won't be sharing that information with us at this point. What we are desperately short of is a witness. They all seem to die.'

....

'Sir, I think we may have a witness.'

'To?'

'Something to do with Birch's movements on the day of his murder.'

'Go on.'

'I went back to Stansted airport. As I said, we didn't find anything on CCTV that was useful – too many individuals fitting the description, impossible to make any visual links or get any information from flight lists. So, we did a bit more on the ground. There was an incident, sir – apparently, there was an issue regarding parking regulations, of all things. A driver tried to use the long stay parking for drop off. There was a bit of a stand-off, the driver insisted his passenger had to get to their flight, the attendant presumably said something along the lines of *so does everyone*, and the driver started to get a bit handy. The attendant called for backup, but by the time he had finished his call the driver had reversed and driven off. Airport police were involved, and bodycam on the attendant got a fair image. They're passing it over, sir.'

'Too good to be true? Any information about the car, or the passenger?'

'Same make and brand, sir. Metallic grey. Didn't get the reg. Just said the passenger was a woman, maybe around 25 years of age.'

'So he was at Stansted airport. Not far from the east coast. Would fit with the location of the murder. Was he followed from the airport? Who was he dropping off? Shame we didn't get more about the car. Wasn't there CCTV at the parking lot?'

'Not in that part of the site, unfortunately.'

'Did you get anything else from the witness?'

'He said he felt the couple were acting a bit strange – looking around, seemed more worried about what was around rather than worrying about cases and documents, which would be the normal situation.'

'It may be useful, Woodley. Even if we just consider it as part of the puzzle, to justify a bit more of the rest. I think we need to get together with OCU, as we may be able to pull in information from the UCO. Can we do anything with the image?'

'I can pass it to forensics, sir. They may be able to do something, even if only to eliminate this man.'
'Fair enough. Let's get it all together.'
....
Superintendent Foale paused, turned to gaze out of the window, and reviewed the information.
'So, we have names for the OCG, we have a possible name for a double agent, we have a possible ID for the formerly unknown body. We have suggestions that there are at least two overseers of proceedings. We have a strong candidate for a collaborator. We have good evidence that Birch was involved on the rescue side and was possibly eliminated by the OCG. What are your plans?'
'We've charged Hardwicke, sir, and are waiting for CPS to confirm approval for detention for trial. He may be able to give us sufficient evidence to be able to locate one or more of the existing OCG members. It might be a bargaining factor.'
'Focus on Hardwicke. I would like an extension for further interviewing before you commit to trial. Get that sorted. He may be able to provide information about the key boss, or bosses. Sounds like the rest are dispensable drones. Make it clear that failing to provide information will inevitably lead to much harsher outcomes. And for goodness' sake get better join up with OCU. Matthews needs to get off his high horse, he's not the Lone Ranger. There may be grounds eventually for handing it over, but for the moment these are two murders, and we're treatment them as such.'
'Sir.'

CHAPTER THIRTEEN *'Some rise by sin, and some by virtue fall.'* (Escalus, *Measure for Measure*)

'You remain under caution, Mr Hardwicke. We have explained to you that the CPS have granted an extension of 48 hours to detain you in order to make further enquiries. Do you understand?'
'Yes.'
'Do you have anything you wish to say at the moment?'
'No.'
'I would make it clear that answering our questions fully and truthfully will make this process much easier for you. You know that you have already admitted to collusion in a serious crime – there isn't really any going back from that, is there? But there is a lot more we need to know about, not just your involvement, but the people you were working with. What can you tell us about them?'
'Not much. One was in charge – he didn't give his name. But he seemed most concerned about getting the job done.'
'How many were there on the day of the drop?'
'Just two. Another man. Didn't seem to speak much English. The one in charge spoke to him in another language.'
'Did you hear either of them use any names?'
'No.'

'I'm sorry, Mr Hardwicke, but I'm a bit confused here. You helped two complete strangers, whose names you didn't know, and who spoke to each other in a different language, to dump a body in the sea? Go back a bit, how did you get to agree to do the job? They just rocked up on the day and one with a bit of English said "would you mind helping us get rid of a body?"?'

'He – the boss – came into the pub, he'd been in contact with the gang who he said wanted a bit of storage work done.'

'And who were they?'

'I don't know – it was one man who did the deals. Didn't give a name. Just agreed the deals.'

'You do live a dangerous life, don't you Mr Hardwicke? Doesn't seem to have got you very far, quite the opposite, in fact. So – the unknown man who did a few deals on the side passed on the fact that you were an easy touch to do a few dodgy jobs for cash, to this other man who wanted to get rid of a body?'

'I just guess they don't like using names.'

'Clearly, according to you. Did you recognise the man who was managing the drop? Had you seen him before?'

Hardwicke paused, and looked to his solicitor, who bent forward and advised him.

'Yes, I had.'

'Ah, interesting! Amazing how memory plays tricks. Where had you seen him?'

'He … came into the pub, it must have been a couple of weeks before.'

'Was he with anyone?'

'Yes – the man who was with him at the drop.'

'I'm starting to feel I can't rely too much on what you say, Mr Hardwicke. I'm just wondering how much you're making up as you go along. If you were able to give us some names, or any information about where these men came from, or anything you know that might help us find them, then it would make a big difference to what happens to you. Do you realise you could be involved in conspiracy to murder charges, or even being accused of the murder itself? Do you know what joint enterprise means and what it entails? Do you know what the inside of a category A prison is like? Do you know what it's like to try and survive years of your life in one?'

Bridgeworth paused, attending to comments relayed from the observation booth from Superintendent Foale.

'But if you can show us exactly what your involvement was, and how much you know about the group, then we can start to look at this situation a bit more realistically. What do you think?'

Hardwicke looked down at his hands clasped on the table, and held the gaze of his solicitor briefly.

'He was called Anton. He told me that if I didn't comply then there would be bad consequences for me.'

'When did he say this?'

'In the pub, a week or so before.'

'Right. What contact had you had with him up to then?'

'He visited a few times, maybe three. After hours. Told me there were plenty of others who would – sort me out – if anything went wrong. Made it clear he was part of a big deal, powerful people. Told me, of course, I mustn't tell anyone, especially the police, or give any information.'

'Of course he did. But if we can find him, and break up the links, we've got a chance of ending what is a dangerous and tragic business. They don't have any qualms about getting rid of anyone who gets in the way.'

He thought of DC Kemble, risking – and giving – her life to do her bit to break the links.

'If we know you are at risk of retribution from these people, then we can take that into account when your case goes to court, which it will. You mentioned Anton – anyone else?'

'He told me the body was that of a man called the Wolf, and that he had killed him.'

Bridgeworth looked across at Woodley.

'Did he say why he had killed him?'

'He betrayed the gang. Put them all at risk. Helped people escape.'

'Did he mention anyone in particular, that the Wolf had helped?'

'Not by name. But the gang killed another man, who knew the Wolf.'

'Why?'

'For that reason – he was trying to break the business. Getting people out.'

'Who?'

'People they had brought from other countries, to work for the gang.'

'People?'

'Women - girls, mainly. There was talk of children, too. But I don't know any details, names or anything.'

'And you don't have any name for this other man?' Hardwicke paused.

'Look, I'm already a marked man. There is no point in me trying to edit what I tell you, or lie to you, because the damage is done, they know. I don't want a lawyer, there's no point. There's only one hope for me, and that's a deal.'

'How?'

'I tell you all I know, and you provide the works – immunity, new identity, house, passport, job.'

'We're not really in the business of making deals, Hardwicke, but I can assure you that we will do everything we can to provide protection if it is deemed in the best interests of all concerned.'

'Then if that's the best I can get, I'm not in any position to argue.

'We have lock-ins sometimes at the pub. Unofficially, we don't notice if money's changing hands. The point is, sometimes it's a great deal of money. In the course of some of the issues that arise, deals get made. I don't usually get involved, but one group worried me, and I tried to break it up. They threatened to report me, get my licence revoked, get me permanently out of a job, worse, unless I gave them a bit of leeway and stepped up to a couple of jobs. At first, I wasn't interested – threats are sometimes part and parcel of the licensing trade – but they were a violent lot, joked a lot about 'cases dealt with', which it turned out involved getting rid of people who got in their way too much. I thought one or two simple jobs wouldn't hurt, especially as they were offering a grand a time. Yes, I know, I should have realised how bad this was. I did a few jobs – picking up items and storing them in the cellar for a bit, 'losing' a few dozen crates. So I didn't think there would be anything wrong in helping them do an unload – if I'd thought about it, I would have realised it was a bit odd – they have plenty of heavies to do that sort of thing – but by now I was getting scared. Maybe it was safer to use someone who was based on the site. I was picking up things – they were talking about "consignments", which it didn't take long to realise were actually women being brought into the country under false pretences and put into the slave trade or prostitution. I thought, one more job and I could get them off my hands. I could move if necessary, go up north, find another pub, before I was forced out.

'The job was to unload "an item" to be picked up by a craft. It seemed simple. But when I offloaded the item, it was clear it was a body. And there was no pickup craft. It was a youngish man, obviously dead a while, unwrapped from a tarp and taken out on a small pontoon and dumped in the sea. The tides should have taken it – him – out. But you need good knowledge of the coast here, it's not just controlled by tides, there are undercurrents, dykes, formations which cause large eddies and backwashes. Turns out he didn't get very far.

'They paid me five grand for that. But I've given back ten times that amount, more, in protection money. Which means I'm broke, which means I'm committed to more jobs. I've had enough. I know too much. But there's no point in trying to recoup it all – if I walk out of here, I won't make it back home.'

'Where can we find Anton?'

'I don't know, but I know who he will probably contact next.'

Bridgeworth paused, without speaking.

'He'll be at the pub. I don't know his name but Anton told me he will send someone to collect the goods soon. I know the pub's closed down now, but they'll be after goods locked up in the back. He'll want to get there before the brewery come to dismantle everything.'

'When?'

'Tonight.'

....

The island was unfamiliar with large-scale night raids by armed police, and the incident caused mixed responses. Younger residents drifted down tentatively to watch proceedings from a distance, while others rushed home, and looked for news on their TVs and iPhones. The operation began covertly, until the pub was surrounded, and a watching brief could be maintained from concealed locations. At around 11.00 p.m., a dirty, unmarked van drove slowly down the lane to the pub, headlights dimmed, and parked in the yard at the back. The covert team held their positions while they waited for the two occupants, armed with jemmies and bolt cutters, to exit the vehicle and head for the barred and padlocked barn behind the property. As soon as they had forced entry, the sudden and tumultuous arrival of a barrage of armed police forced them to drop their tools and reach for their weapons.

....

By early morning, two prisoners arrived at headquarters, were booked in and detained. They spoke little English, and by the time an interpreter had been located and had read them their rights, it was 5.00 a.m. They were left in their cells to rest until the morning shift arrived, to arrange new interpreters for their first interviews.

....

Matthews and Harris introduced themselves via the interpreters and began a slow and wearying interview of the first man, who gave his name as Radek Janota.

'You were arrested on the count of breaking and entering a property. Why were you there?'

'I was being paid to, by my boss.'

'His or her name?'

'Jakub Rusu.'

'What did he pay you to do?'

'To get anything I could find there.'

'Anything in particular?'

'I don't know … anything we could find.'

'How would you know what to get?'

'It didn't matter – Jakub said pick up anything you can.'

'Who is Jakub Rusu?'

'I worked for him.'

'I know, but what does he do?'

'He is dead now. But we were told we must continue.'

'By whom?'

'I don't know. It was one of the big bosses. They told us.'

The interview continued in a slow and sporadic manner, and was repeated by the other individual, who gave his name as Anton Masin.

Matthews and Harris compared their notes.

'It's frustrating, because we know they must be part of the gang, but we've arrested them for breaking and entering. Without more evidence, there's nothing more we can charge them with. I doubt we'll get an extension on what we have at the moment. We know their names are linked with the Rusus and we know they're very probably part of the OCG, but we just have their names at the moment, nothing more. Other than that both Rusus are dead now, so there must be someone higher up the chain.'

'Can we not use their activity to link them with the OCG, sir? We've got the evidence from CID that Hardwicke knew they were coming, and knew they were from the OCG.'

'They were *sent* by the OCG, they weren't *from* the OCG, on the evidence we have. We're justified only in asking what they know about the Rusu connection. And they're denying knowledge, obviously. We'll charge them for now then look at whether we can commit them for trial. We can do some covert intel. What do the usual checks show?'

'Nothing on our records, sir. Prints negative. I don't know if we're justified in going international?'

'Very unlikely. Probably illegally in the country but again that's not the reason for the arrest. It's unfortunately the case that we just have to look at resources, which won't give us much to take it further. There's an outside chance this won't even go to court. But if it does, it's not likely to be a custodial. Which does mean we can keep tabs on them a bit I suppose, if it comes to that. But this may be a magistrates' court issue only, maybe fines. I'm not hopeful we can go any further than this. We need more.'
....
Bridgeworth knocked on the office door.
Matthews looked up, making effort to contain his irritation.
'What can I do for you, John?'
'I heard you'd made two arrests? The OCG case?'
'We did – thanks to your Hardwicke information.'
'Anything come out of it?'
'We got them for breaking and entering, that's about it.'
'How come?'
'Sorry?'
'It was an OCU op, wasn't it?'
'They both denied involvement.'
'Of course they did – but can't you get anything on them?'
'Without evidence, no.'
'But I've got a witness, Robert. Hardwicke. Can you let me have just one go with the two you've got, before the 24 hours is up?'
'You haven't got a witness, John. He didn't see them.'
'Didn't he?'
Matthews gazed at him, realising he had no case to argue, and that Hardwicke wasn't even his witness.
'Go ahead. I don't see any problem in interviewing them as part of the Hardwicke case. You might not get the interpreters in time, though.'
'Oh, I think I can have a go. Thanks for the loan of your prisoners.'
....

Superintendent Foale glanced up as John Matthews entered.

'Come on in, John. Take a seat, no formalities. I must say I'm very interested in what you've come up with. I know DCI Hammond didn't want the lines blurred, and I fully understand that. I've no intention of questioning his judgement there. But - and I will be frank here, this is unofficial - I think we can ignore the line for the moment, based on what you've told me here.'

He referred to a document on the desk.

'You know I'm not one to single anyone out, John. But I can't help thinking you've gone above and beyond. In a good way. Tell me your thoughts.'

'I recognise there may have been some - redundancy - in our investigations, sir, and I apologise for that. But the incident with the raid on the pub …'

'It's OK, John - I consider it to be … ill-advised?'

'Well, sir, it seemed like the plan shot itself in the foot. So much more could have been achieved if the command had been delayed. In my view, sir. And I realise that the two arrests were based on a limited charge. But I felt there was all the more reason to have one last go, keeping it in the confines of the charge, of course, sir.'

'I agree, John, but we need to be careful. Although the outcome has taken us much further forward in getting access to information. To put it mildly. Good work - but time for CID to pull out of it for now, we can deal with the rest. At the very least we can give the family of Birch more to perhaps help them deal with it, which is no small part of our job. Get back to work, John. Next job waiting, I'm sure.'

'Thank you, sir.'

…….

'Mr Janota, I understand your boss is a man called Jakub Rusu? Is he a good boss?'

'He was OK.'

'Was?'

'He is dead now. I don't know how.'

'How long had you known him?'

'I don't know …'

'A week? A month? Six months?'

"Six months – maybe – yes.'

'He must have been a good boss, then. Did he pay you well?'

'I don't know … yes …'

'So you did quite a lot for Jakub, it sounds? But now he's gone, who do you work for?'

'Why are you asking me all these questions about my boss? I have told the other man everything I know.'

'Because it's quite a big deal, to drive from London to the coast to burgle a large property, armed, when you don't know who or what might be there. I'm sure there is more you can tell me.'

The man stayed silent.

'If I were a criminal, I don't think I would take that sort of chance unless I knew more about the job.'

The man continued to stay silent.

'I'm not getting much from you, Mr Janota. I'm a bit concerned you may be worried about the job? Was it the first time you went there? Or had you been there before, so knew the lay of the land, if you like – knew what you were taking on?'

'I can't say.'

'Why can you not say, Mr Janota? Are you frightened of your boss? Will he be angry that you didn't complete the job, in fact that you got arrested?'

The man looked panicked, his eyes wide.

'Please, you must protect me.'

'Well, we don't normally offer protection unless there is good reason, Mr Janota. Is there good reason?'

'They will kill me, both of us. If I leave this station, I will be dead.'

'I don't believe this is about not finishing the job, Radek. I believe you are involved with an organised crime group, and have been for some time. And I believe we would be able to offer some protection if you would give us as much information as you know about the gang and its business, who's running it, where it can be found. It's your only hope really, Mr Janota.'

'If I tell you, you will protect me?'

'If we feel it is in the best interests, we will offer you some protection. There are going to be complications, if you are in the country illegally. But I assure you we will do our best to sort that out.'

'Who are the bosses?'

…….

'I really appreciate you giving up your day off, Woodley. We've got to deal with this straight away, before we run out of time.'

'Of course, sir. What's been happening?'

'I knew it. OCU have messed up. They set up an op to catch two of the gang attempting to get the stuff from the pub. They got them on breaking and entering – breaking and entering, what the …! Come on! I managed to get Matthews to let me see them. Played the *I've got the witness* card. Just saw one of them, and I think it's enough to rescue this before we lose the source – if Janota gets out of here, we'll never see him again, and not because he makes a clever escape.

'I know what's been going on. I was trying to understand it all - the business of the triangle; the involvement of Hardwicke; the two UCOs - Caroline and another; who was in the gang, who was in the rescue group - then when I decided to cut out the detail, was almost giving up on it - I knew.

'Listen to this. You remember Cisar and Keiser? Who turn out to be the bosses, not surprisingly (thanks to your interest in translation). You said that Cisar was Czech and Visser was Dutch for leader, emperor. So that turns out to be correct. But listen to this …'

Matthews started the recording.

'… sort that out. Who are the bosses?'

'There are two bosses – they're known as Cisar and Keizer. They run the entire operation jointly, from Amsterdam and Prague. They are powerful men, two of the leading crime bosses in Europe. One was in charge of running the gangs, making links and connections, finding sources and supplies. The other headed up the rescue organisation. This way they both had complete control of the whole set-up. But they will never allow themselves to be known to be linked.'

'Do you know their real names?'

'I do. Bucek and Visser.'

'I think I'd made that connection, Radek. I take it Bucek ran the rescue operation, and Visser the gangs?'

'Oh no, sir. It was Bucek who ran the gangs. Visser was in charge of running the rescue operation. They informed each other all the time, but without any knowledge by the outside world.'

'But Bucek …'

'Yep. Bucek was the very helpful and hospitable one, but Visser wouldn't have anything to do with us, maintaining that plan to keep their relationship well out of the public eye; and then two British cops turn up and ask them both for information about the same thing! What's the saying, keep your friends close, but keep you enemies closer? That Prague hotel is losing its happy place in my memory, Woodley.

'I knew it before I knew it, if you know what I mean. That visit to Prague, it rankled somehow. Bucek, in the guise of trying to give us helpful information, in fact gave us everything we needed to know. A double bluff, if you like. He mentioned political corruption and bribery being their major "challenge". He talked about infiltrators, collaborators, perpetrators. He diverted us very cleverly to Visser, who he suggested was actually unlikely to see us and therefore - by implication - was involved in the business. He wanted us to trust him and suspect Visser. He was even smug about trying to control the activities. He knew the body was untraceable but gave us little titbits to confuse us. He completely sideswiped us with an embarrassing degree of generosity.

'And we - I - made the rookie error of looking into the situation from just one perspective - that, basically, Bucek was on our side. He was giving it to us on a plate.

'So, listen, there's more -

'Tell me about the Rusus.'

'They are both dead, sir.'

'How did Jakub die?'

' Jakub was killed by Vulpe. This all meant we had to deal only with Bucek. He is the one who decides who will die. Vulpe not only was a traitor, but he killed one of the most important members of the gang.'

'So Jakub was killed before the drop was made?'

'Which is probably why the plans began to fall apart. With Gregor killed in the fire, and Jakub murdered, the gang became reckless, out of control.'

'The names on the lists, sir?'

'Well, we know the names on one list were accurate in terms of the OCG members. We now know who Keizer and Cisar were, and we know they were linked with Andrei Vulpe, who was collaborating with the AAS. And of course that Kyle was Birch. By the way, Hana - another member of the group - was Caroline herself.'

'X and Y?'

'I'll come to that.'

'What do we do with that information, sir?'

'I don't know yet, Woodley. I'll speak to the Super. But the X and Y brings me to another issue, which I'll go back to later. Meanwhile, the interview was past the watershed by that time and Janota was pretty happy to give me information about the current location, in return for full protection, and dealing with potential deportation. This operation is costing us a pretty penny, but there you go. That I'm happy to pass to OCU – for now. Meanwhile, it's our job to tie up the two deaths.'

'So the island body was Vulpe?'

'Vulpe? Yes, it was an alias, but also a risky one. The wolf's head or fox's head was a known symbol for the rescue group, but in Vulpe's case it was a very unfortunate coincidence - he had a fox's head tattooed on just because it matched his name. So the tattoos were also risky, but both were pre-existing, and he had to hope the relevance was not noted. He probably managed to keep them covered when necessary. Janota said Vulpe received word of a brother coming to the UK to find his sister. His remit from the rescue group was to deter him at all odds. An outsider would put the rescue operation at risk. The password for Kyle had been the Dutch for 'purple donkey', and this was the item which the brother gave to Vulpe. This was to be used instead of the password. Unfortunately, again, this never reached Kyle, who was to take it to the woman, Johanna. Vulpe was eliminated the night that he met Jan, the brother. The toy was taken from the pouch and destroyed.

'Vulpe was locked in a garage for several days, bleeding from the wounds to his hands, provided only with syringes of heroin, no food or water. It is presumed he lost teeth in drugged falls into items in the garage, or as the result of blows inflicted by the gang.

'Eventually, his body was collected from the lockup, and taken to the coast, to appear as a possible failed immigration attempt, or assault.

'Presumably he died from his injuries, so we'll never know who was responsible for his death. We don't fully understand how that happened, but we are pretty sure that he was the double agent. I guess it's a point in his favour, that he risked his life, to try and undo some of the work he had been involved in.'

'Fair enough. As they say, not all criminals set out to be one.'

'Doesn't apply in the eyes of the law, I'm afraid. I think his fate was set, by whatever means.'

'So, Birch?'

'Birch became involved in the group working to help victims, firstly remotely, via a closed Facebook group under a different name, then by offering to put in some practical help.

'He became a carrier for the AAS. The evidence from the USB stick was information regarding his next job. 'Jane' was the name he was given of his passenger. He must have mentioned this to his sister, in passing – maybe to create a diversion, to suggest he was in a relationship.

'He became tasked with rescue pickups. The 'warning' on the note was to be aware that the task was high risk. He used the name Kyle for identification, to safeguard his own identity. He was given the identifying rosary through careful mediation by our UCO. Unfortunately, presumably he left it at his flat in his haste, and never got to return it. His role was to oversee the process of collecting Johanna and following through the support necessary to get her to the airport. Which he did, despite nearly being scuppered by a disagreement regarding parking – who hasn't been there? – but maybe not well enough to evade members of the gang who tracked him. So, he was ambushed and killed on his return journey from the airport.

'It's going to liaison with OCU to solve that one.'

'Where does Frank Beckswith come in? Could he have been involved in any part of it?'

'Very unlikely, Woodley. Frank Beckswith doesn't exist. He was X. Or rather, the man who was described as Beckswith was actually the other UCO. Good back story though - I liked the used car salesman idea. If you've ever met DS Pat Hopkins, you'll know why I think that.'

'And the other thing?'

'Sorry?'

'You said you were going to go back to it.'

'Ah. Do you remember the triangle? Bucek, the instigator and leader, to organise; Vulpe, to put it all in place, make it work; and one other, to manage information and communication. Remember how Bucek was just a bit too helpful, and dropped hints about Visser knowing more? And Visser wouldn't see us – not because he was the one at the top, but because he was frightened of the one, or ones, at the top. Bucek wanted Visser to look like the corrupt one, deflecting suspicion away from himself, telling us so much about the clues. So Bucek was part of the overriding management, and Vulpe got the job done. Visser wasn't actually part of the triangle. So, we have Bucek, running the business, and Vulpe doing the dirty work.'

'So who was in charge of information and communication then?'

'Information is valuable. A policeman's salary is never going to provide for the high life, is it? A generous payout from a corrupt but successful organisation might well do that. Organised crime pockets millions - maybe billions - every year. Who would know that? A member of OCU, certainly. And DS Harris was drawn to the half million, garnered by corruption in high places, that would be earned by revealing the existence and presence of undercover officers. He was the other corner of the triangle. That's one decision Matthews might be regretting for a while.'

CHAPTER FOURTEEN. *'The fault, dear Brutus, is not in our stars but in ourselves.'* (Cassius, Julius Caesar)

In a small corner of Olsanske Cemetery, a young woman knelt down on the earth facing a rough, unmarked wooden cross. She knew this was next to the Palacek family grave, and that there were none left to attend further to the site. She leant forward, and gently touched the earth. Andrei was the last; adopted after the death of his parents in the uprisings in the years between the Prague Spring and the Velvet Revolution. She knew he had always fought for what was right; it must have been in his blood. It certainly did not suit the strict fundamentalist family who accepted him, which led to his escape into the reactionary groups of the underground movements. He never wanted to be part of murder, only of revolution and change. She knew this was sadly large part of the history of beautiful Prague. So many had died for their efforts, after becoming embroiled in the intensity of revolution. He would be happier here, lying next to his true family, his real parents. It was sad that he would not be honoured for his beliefs and commitment. But it was nice that the horse chestnut trees above were beginning to blossom with huge clusters of white, pink and yellow flowers.

....
Some 800 miles away from Olsanske, a very different commemoration was taking place.

Margaret Birch and her daughter had invited relatives to the memorial service, but not knowing of her son's life outside his work did not have access to his circle of friends. The service, then, was small and private, in the chapel of St Augustine's.

The chapel seated some 60 people at a stretch. It struggled to accommodate the crowd which stood respectfully at the sides and rear of the chapel and left many more quietly standing in the still garden beyond.

Margaret leant closer to her daughter, anxious about the unexpected demand to engage with so many unknown and disparate people - some, she felt, looked a little disreputable. But her anxiety was misplaced, as at the end of the brief service all that remained were the flowers which lay like a shower of blossom beyond the door.
....
The evening light over the Rhine cast delicate, shifting patterns over the quiet revellers on the banks.

At a table in a bright and busy bar, a couple sat, a bottle of wine between them.

'Do you think it's the wisest thing to do?'

'I don't know, but it's my choice. It has taken a long time to come to terms with what happened, and I wouldn't say I'm anything like the same as I was before. But I don't want to live alone, being someone I'm not, for the sake of hoping I won't be found. I just don't fear that any more. I nearly died, and what else is there to fear greater than that? I want my life back, to be with my family, start thinking about a better future.'

'I'm glad. You know I will do anything to help.'

'Look, I will never be able to pay back what I owe you. You risked your life, many times I think, but you didn't stop.'

'But in the end, you didn't actually need me.'

The woman fixed her gaze on the man.

'I needed you from day one. From the day you tried to stop me, I knew you were there, I knew you wouldn't give up, and it's people like you who made it possible. I thank every one of them. If I had thought more carefully before …'

'No. It's the way it is. But it's not our place to intervene any more. We have to trust the police.'

'I hope so.'

'What will you do now?'

'I've got a great job. Working for a publishing company. In Amsterdam, fortunately. I hope it will lead on to good things. It pays well. And I want to make up for all the worry and stress.'

'Oh - look, I've got something for you. No, it's not a purple donkey! I don't think you'd ever want a model donkey again! It's this.'

'He drew from his pocket a rosary, made of delicate rose pink stones interspersed with siler filigree links.

'How did you get that?'

'I spoke to the police. They were relaxed about it. Once all the documentation had been put right, and I could prove you were my sister, they were happy for me to take it. It was no longer of value as evidence, and in the circumstances it would be difficult for them to give it you directly, or for you to collect it. I don't think Oma would have been too happy for it to stay in some dusty cupboard in a British police station.'

'I think she would be proud of the journey it's had. And now it's back safe with its home. You don't stop, do you?''

'And now, we're going to do even more – we're going to order from this amazing menu, then I'm taking you home, to meet Mila, who hopefully you will approve for a future sister-in-law, who knows? And if you don't – well, let's just say I won't place too much importance on your judgement …'

She threw a gentle tap across to his shoulder.

'Shut up! But I guess I deserve that! And for that you can pay for this meal!'

The unusually warm Spring sun began to sleep on the horizon, and the lights over the river began slowly to come to life.

....

It was pleasant to sit out on the small terrace outside her cottage on the warm, summer evening. It was almost a year since events on the island had taken something of a dramatic turn. She knew she hadn't quite recovered – she didn't like to linger too long on the sea wall; but was determined she wouldn't be deterred from the enjoyment of her walks and the peace of the island. She had been reassured that she had nothing of value to interest the criminals involved – the only person who might have held a grudge was not going to cause her any problems now, even if he were able to identify her as the witness. The Ship was run by a very pleasant new couple, in their forties, with two teenage sons, who seemed sensible. The mother had already heard that she was a retired teacher and was thinking of asking her advice about her eldest son's upcoming A level choices. The atmosphere in the pub was different, too. It felt more authentic, she thought. A genuine coastal pub, with good seafood and Essex beer, rather than a slightly phoney old seafarers' watering hole. Gail had even suggested she could come and visit again for a few days – in Gail's practical and slightly ironic way, a kind of anniversary … marking? Not really a celebration. But they would definitely take the same walk, probably as a sort of act of defiance. Life goes on.

....

John Bridgeworth was not the type to philosophise about his job, or even about life in general. It never turned out well, in his experience. He had a job to do, and he either did it well, or he didn't. And what happened if he got too cocky about it, was that the job would turn round and bite him in the face. But in this case, compared with some of the people involved, he felt he'd got the job done, at least. Alan Woodley came through the door of the pub, somewhat flustered.

'Sorry, sir – forgot it was Cary's birthday. Had to stop off and get some flowers. Can't stay long – promised I'd book a table. Can I get you a pint?'

'A quick one would be welcome, Alan. Wouldn't want to get in the way of your family celebrations. But I thought it would be good to catch up out of the office.'

....

'So what's the update, sir?'

Bridgeworth had managed to have the use of a back room at the pub, and the space was quiet, separated from the main bar by a deep, 18th century stone wall.

'Hardwicke's evidence led to the arrest of Bucek and Visser, for further investigation. Bucek will probably be charged with corruption in office, solicitation for the purposes of enforced prostitution, and conspiracy to murder - that all suggests a pretty tough sentence. I wouldn't be surprised if he gets life. Visser has already been charged with deception and dereliction of duty. He received a suspended sentence and was dismissed from the force. Presumably this is one nail in the coffin of the OCG, although it will have plenty more candidates for the job, I'm sure. Hardwicke has got off pretty lightly, but I don't think he'll be running a pub any more. I expect he'll be looking over his shoulder for a while. He'll be in special protection. A new identity and location is enough for him; he'll have to deal with the rest himself. Masin has been deported, to face trial in the Czech Republic. Because Janota gave crucial evidence, his immigration status was reviewed and he was granted three years' asylum in the UK with additional conditions. We've provided enough information to support some leniency in the sentencing of both of them.'

'Harris?'

'Charged with corruption and misconduct. Got the maximum five years, owing to the seriousness of the crime. He also got seven years for involvement in the crime of human trafficking, to run concurrently. But to be honest I don't think the legal bit matters too much. Any period in a Cat A or B for an ex-police officer is frankly not worth thinking about. No point in analysing it, though. His choice.'

'Matthews?'

'Moved down to DS in Ops. Lucky to get away with that, frankly. At least he won't be responsible for too much decision-making, I suppose.'

'Sorry, sir.'

'What do you mean?'

'Well – it's depressing, isn't it?'

'It's the way that it is. Drink up, Cary's waiting. Enjoy the meal.'

'We will, sir. See you in the morning.'

'Will do.'

Bridgeworth breathed in a few moments of silence, before the warmth and chatter from the main bar began to filter through to the back room, as the evening custom increased in number. He was getting a bit old for this, he thought. He realised he was starting to philosophise, and saw this as a sign that it really might be time to think about looking again at that email about early retirement. Or not. He went to get another pint.

40087 201221

Printed in Dunstable, United Kingdom

73754490R00084